The EXPLODING Life of Scarlett Fife

The EXPLODING Life of Scarlett Fife

MaZ EVanS

ILLUSTRATED BY CHRIS JEVONS

HODDER

HODDER CHILDREN'S BOOKS

First published in Great Britain in 2021 by Hodder and Stoughton

1 3 5 7 9 10 8 6 4 2

Text copyright © Maz Evans, 2021
Illustrations copyright © Chris Jevons, 2021

The moral rights of the author and illustrator have been asserted.

A CIP catalogue record for this book
is available from the British Library.

ISBN 978 1 444 95767 9
WTS ISBN 978 1 444 96420 2

Printed and bound in Great Britain by
Clays Ltd, Elcograf S.p.A

The paper and board used in this book
are made from wood from responsible sources.

MIX
Paper from
responsible sources
FSC® C104740

Hodder Children's Books
An imprint of
Hachette Children's Group
Part of Hodder and Stoughton
Carmelite House
50 Victoria Embankment
London EC4Y 0DZ

An Hachette UK Company
www.hachette.co.uk

www.hachettechildrens.co.uk

For Veronique

Who regularly stops me from exploding.

Thank you for being my clay pot.
Xxx

Scarlett

Maisie

Polly

Ms Pitt-Bull

Aunty Amara   Aunty Rosa

William U and his Mum

Emmeline

Jakub

Gran

Rita

Bruce

CHAPTER 1

I AM SO ANGRY I THINK MY BUM MIGHT FALL OFF!!!!

Mr Nibbles was mine!!! Mine!!! Not stupid William U's!!!! Mine!!!!

Here is a pie chart that proves how much I want Mr Nibbles:

Things I Really Want

3% ALL THE PLASTIC OUT OF THE OCEAN

32% A UNIMINGO CHANGEY SEQUIN JUMPER

100000000000000000% MR NIBBLES

11% JAKUB TO FIND HIS JOB

And I don't even care that this pie chart doesn't actually add up to a hundred per cent like pie charts actually should. (*Which I'd normally really care about, by the way, because that's how pie charts work and that's why I'm on The Purple Table in Maths, which we all know is the best one, but we have to pretend that all the Maths tables are the same, even though The Green Table still haven't learned their three times table and probably think a pie chart is a menu in a cafe.*) THAT'S how much I **WANT MR NIBBLES!!**

(*By the way, I really want Mr Nibbles.*)

Let me explain something:

Mr Nibbles is Rainbow Class's pet hamster and

everyone at St Lidwina's Primary School loves him (*except for Vashti because she says it's important to be an individual, which is why she never brushes her hair*).

Every week, everyone really wants to get the most Positivity Points so they can be Star of the Week and look after Mr Nibbles for the weekend.

I REALLY wanted Mr Nibbles to come home with me this weekend, so I have been **EXTRA SUPER MEGA GOOD**.

To get the most Positivity Points, I have:

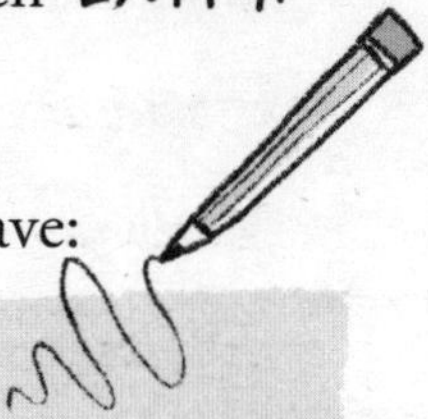

- Sharpened all the pencils at playtime *(even though Darcy had the new UniMingo hairbrush and she said it was my turn to try it at playtime after Milly and Roshin, but only if Milly didn't have nits any more like she did at Parva's hair-braiding party and we all got them and school had to send A Letter Home).*
- Said thank you *all* the time *(even when I didn't mean it, like when the dinner ladies put broccoli on my plate, because the only place broccoli should EVER be put is in vegetable prison).*
- Learned my eight times tables backwards

(although I wanted to do that because Maths is my favourite and I'm really good at it, which is why I'm on The Purple Table).

 Helped to clean up the dinner hall after lunchtime *(even though it looked like the bottom of the monkey enclosure at a wildlife park after the monkeys had a party and then had to leave calmly and quietly for a fire alarm).*

This was what the top of the Positivity Chart looked like when I got to school this morning:

SCARLETT: 29
MATTHEW: 27
MAISIE: 25
WILLIAM U: 24
VASHTI: 23

(I was a bit worried when Vashti got four Positivity

Points for actually brushing her hair for the school photo, but she broke Darcy's UniMingo hairbrush doing it, so the points came right back off again.)

Mr Nibbles was mine. I was all ready for him and even made a special Mr Nibbles area in my bedroom with:

* A bed.
* A bath.
* An obstacle course *(I don't want him to get bored).*
* A book *(in case he wakes up in the night with bad dreams and can't sleep).*
* A night light *(I don't want him to be scared and wake up with bad dreams).*
* A teddy *(which I took out because it was bigger than him and I thought it might give him bad dreams despite the night light and then he might not like the book to get back to sleep).*

I was **SUPER EXCITED** because I've never

had Mr Nibbles before …

And then this afternoon I went to the Positivity Chart to see:

WILLIAM U: 32

SCARLETT: 29

MATTHEW: 27

VASHTI: 26 *(She borrowed someone else's brush for the school photo.)*

MAISIE: 25

… and William U standing smugly next to Mr Nibbles's cage. 'WHAT?????!!!!' I shouted. EIGHT POSITIVITY POINTS? HOW DID YOU GET EIGHT

POSITIVITY POINTS? When the dinner ladies accidentally set the fish fingers on fire, the firefighters who saved the school didn't get **EIGHT POSITIVITY POINTS!** How did you ...?'

But then I followed his smug look in the direction of Mrs Underwood. Our teaching assistant.

And also William U's mum.

Let me explain something:

William U *always* gets Mr Nibbles. William U *always* gets everything he wants. And if William U doesn't get what he wants, William U's mum *always* gets it for him.

William U *always* gets loads of Positivity Points and has *never* been on The Cloud for making bad choices, even though he should live on The Cloud because he's super mean to everyone, but especially me because:

1) I'm much better than William U at Maths and he likes to be best at everything.

2) The one time William U came to my house for a playdate, he tried to pull the head off my UniMingo slippers and I told on him and my mum told his mum and although he never gets in trouble with his mum, he's never forgiven me for telling on him.

3) William U probably can't think of a third thing because I'm better than him at Maths.

(By the way, William U isn't to be confused with William D who can name all the dinosaurs and once ate a snail, even though William D WASN'T in France and the snail WAS in his garden.)

William U's mum used to work as a lawyer with my Aunty Rosa (*which is how bogie-head William U got invited to her engagement party, so I've got to see him tonight as WELL as all day at school*). Aunty Rosa told me that William U's mum used to get upset about people not getting paid enough, and people being treated unfairly, and people's human rights not being respected.

But then William U's mum gave up being a lawyer and had William U. So now William U's mum mainly gets upset about What Upset William.

On sports day, What Upset William was Felix beating him in the running race and getting a Special Sticker. William U's mum said that William U had Competition Aversion Syndrome so he should get a Special Sticker just for taking part. (*By the way, William U's mum says William U has lots of syndromes. Some of them are so new that the doctors don't even know about them. But William U's mum finds them on www.MyChildCentre.Universe and that makes them true.*) But then What Upset William was that he only wanted Felix's gold Special Sticker, so William U's mum said that William U had Selective Sticker Syndrome and made Felix swap with him.

A few months ago, What Upset William was our old teaching assistant, Mr Chance, threatening to put William U on The Cloud for scribbling on Maisie's poem about worms. William U's mum (*who is also a school governor and head of the PTA, by the way*) told our old head teacher that not only was William U allergic to worm poems (*William U is allergic to everything, by the way, including green vegetables, homework, sitting next to Freddie and Spanish*), but that maybe it would be a good idea if William U's mum became Rainbow Class's teaching assistant instead of Mr Chance and also would the school like the PTA to buy every class a new laptop?

So this week, What Upset William was me getting Mr Nibbles. William U's mum said he had Hamster Co-Dependency Syndrome and gave him EIGHT POSITIVITY POINTS for sharpening the pencils, which was TOTALLY unfair because when I sharpened the pencils, she only gave me THREE POSITIVITY POINTS.

I went to ask my teacher Miss Hugg about it, but William U's mum came over and, although I couldn't hear exactly what they were talking about, William U's mum whispered something about Miss Hugg's application to the governors for a 'celery increase'. (*Which is weird, by the way – why would anyone want more celery? It should be in the cell next to broccoli in vegetable prison.*) Then Miss Hugg went very quiet and William U got Mr Nibbles and I got some BIG FEELINGS about it.

Let me explain something:

I am 135 cm and weigh 26 kg. Sometimes my

feelings must be at least 136 cm and weigh over 27 kg because they just don't fit inside me: these are my BIG FEELINGS. They bubble up inside me and before I can do anything about them, they come out of my mouth. The angry BIG FEELINGS get me in quite a lot of trouble, but I really can't help it. I have especially BIG FEELINGS about William U getting Mr Nibbles when it was my turn.

It's now playtime and I am SUPER ANGRY and I can feel the bubbles of angry in my tummy. But Maisie (*who, by the way, is my best forever friend in the whole wide world*) is telling me to 'Just Calm Down'. Telling someone to 'Just Calm Down' when they are angry is like telling someone to 'just hold it in' when they really need a wee. It's going to come out no matter what anyone says (*but at least with angry feelings you don't have to go home with your tights in a Special Bag like Milly did after the Year 2 Christmas disco*).

'Scarlett,' Maisie says calmly, 'you need to get some perspective.'

Maisie talks a lot about perspective, which she says is about looking differently at something. Maisie always has a different perspective. Maybe it's because she doesn't have a mum and dad and she's grown up with lots of foster families. Or maybe it's because she wears red glasses.

'You just have to accept it,' Maisie says. 'William U is Star of the Week. It's *a feta company.*'

'What does that mean?' I ask her.

'It's French for "nothing you can do about it",' Maisie explains *(by the way, Maisie is super good at words, even in different languages).* 'So you didn't get Mr Nibbles? Think of all the children who don't have enough to eat, or don't have a home to live in.'

So I think about all the children who don't have enough to eat or a home to live in and now I feel really angry for them and I still don't have

Mr Nibbles this weekend, so I kick the climbing frame, which makes me fall over and now I have a sore foot and a sore bum, those children still don't have enough to eat or homes to live in, and I STILL DON'T HAVE MR NIBBLES, so I'm just going to shout a bit.

'I think your perspective needs a little more work,' Maisie says quietly as I yell on the playground floor.

Maybe I need to get red glasses too.

Chapter 1+1

It's my aunties' engagement party tonight and I'm still SUPER angry. I told my mum and Jakub about Mr Nibbles and the Positivity Points and William U's Hamster Co-Dependency Syndrome in the car on the way to Aunty Rosa's Big Posh House.

'So that's what William's got now,' sighed my mum, giving Jakub The Look that meant she didn't want to say Something Not Appropriate in front of me, like, 'Actually, I think William U has Stinky Bum-Head Syndrome,' which was what we were all thinking anyway, so she might as well have said it.

So I said it instead.

'I think William U has Stinky Bum-Head Syndrome,' I grumble.

'Scarlett – that's Not Appropriate,' Mum said, giving Jakub the Look that meant she completely agreed with me.

'It's not fair!' I shouted. 'I had the most Positivity Points! I should be Star of the Week! Mr Nibbles should be at the engagement party with *me*!'

Mum and Jakub laughed.

'Oh, pickle,' Jakub said with a smile. 'This would never happen! No parent in their right mind would let a child bring a hamster to an engagement party!'

An hour later, I am watching William U play with Mr Nibbles at the engagement party.

'My William's struggling with Parental Denial Discontentment Syndrome,' William U's mum whispers to mine as she looks proudly at William feeding Mr Nibbles some ham and cheese quiche straight from the buffet table (*William U's mum always calls William U 'my William', by the way, which is weird because it's not like anyone else would want him*).

'I do not understand this?' Jakub asks. English is Jakub's second language as he was born in Poland. Sometimes he needs to ask about English words, because English words don't always make sense to him. I *totally* understand that because English words don't always make sense to me either and I wasn't born in Poland. Numbers make sense:

$$1 + 1 = 2$$
$$18 - 3 = 15$$
$$8 \times 8 = 64$$

(*I remember the last one, by the way, by saying, 'I ate and I ate until I was sick on the floor, eight times eight equals sixty-four.*)

But words don't always make sense and too many words sound like too many other words. When Mum told me when I was six that 'Jakub's going to be your stepdaddy', I thought we were going to use him to get into the loft.

'So what is this "Parental Denial Discontentment Syndrome"?' Jakub asks William U's mum.

'Oh, it's very new,' says William U's mum seriously. 'There's a whole thread about it on www. MyChildCentre.Universe. It's when a child has an extremely negative response to not being allowed something.'

'Ah yes – I had this same condition as a child,' Jakub says, eating a huge piece of quiche. (*Jakub is always eating, by the way. He can fit two crumpets in his mouth at once – FACT.*) 'I got very cross when my mother refused to allow me to watch television late on a school night.'

'Really?' says William U's mum, looking actually surprised. 'What did she do?'

'Sent me to my room and told me not to come out until I'd stopped being such a spoiled baby,' Jakub says. 'It was very good medicine.'

Mum spits out some of her Bubbly Mummy

Juice. William U's mum looks as if she has some **BIG FEELINGS** about Jakub but then walks away to make sure Nothing Is Upsetting William.

'Emi, darling,' booms a voice behind Mum. Jakub jumps. My granny always makes Jakub jump. My granny makes a lot of people jump, but not me because she's my granny and always gives me sweets. Mum says it's because she's 'formidable', which means someone who makes people jump.

'Hi, Mum,' says my mum, giving Granny a kiss. 'How are you? How are you feeling?'

'Pah!' says Granny, giving me a big cuddle. 'It was nothing. Doctors making a big fuss over a silly cold.'

'It was pneumonia,' says Mum quietly. 'You need to look after yourself, Mum.'

'Poppycock,' mutters Granny, drinking a big glass of red wine. (*My granny was born in the 1940s, so uses lots of words from the olden days, like 'poppycock', 'balderdash' and 'video recorder'. It's very cute.*)

Let me explain something:

Unlike William U, there is *never* anything wrong with my granny. Last year she was taken to hospital after she fell over. She told the doctors that all she needed was a couple of pills and a plaster. They told her that she'd had a heart attack. She was back at her job teaching at the university two weeks later.

'We'd better go through to the other room,' says Jakub. 'They are doing the speeches soon I think.'

'Sure,' hiccoughs my mum. 'I'm just going to pay a little visit.'

(By the way, that means she needs the toilet. You see? Words make no sense. Once Jakub asked her if 'paying a little visit' meant the same as 'going for a wee or a poo'. She said yes, it did – and could they please finish the conversation when we weren't in the middle of the cinema.)

The adults go through to the lounge (*Aunty*

20

Rosa's Big Posh House is so big and posh, by the way, she has a sitting room, a living room, a lounge and a 'snug', which all do exactly the same thing, but make it great for hide and seek), where Aunty Rosa's vicar, Reverend Wright, is going to make a speech about Aunty Rosa and her fiancée, Aunty Amara.

Aunty Amara is **SUPER** nice – she's a creative therapist, which means she helps people to express their feelings through art. She met my Aunty Rosa (*who is my mum's little sister, by the way*) when Aunty Rosa went on a stress management course. Aunty Amara suggested that Aunty Rosa make a clay pot to release her stress through pottery. Aunty Rosa hates pottery, so she released her stress by squishing her pot, which she said made her feel much less stressed. Then she and Aunty Amara fell in love, which made her loads less stressed, at least until she started planning a wedding.

'Where is the band?' Aunty Rosa huffs, coming

up behind Mum. 'They were supposed to be here at six. Hey, squidge.'

She gives me a quick hug, then goes back to looking around for anyone who looks as if they might be in a band.

'Calm down,' says Mum, who always acts like Aunty Rosa's big sister, even though they're both really old now and I'm not sure anyone knows the difference any more.

'*Calm down*,' says Aunty Rosa in a silly voice before poking my mum. She always acts like my mum's little sister and it's very funny. Mum says Aunty Rosa is 'immature', which is strange because even though Aunty Rosa is younger than my mum, she has a Big Posh House and lots more money. I once asked my mum if she minded that her younger sister had a Big Posh House and lots more money than her. Mum said that she didn't and we never needed to have that conversation again, so that was good.

'Relax,' says Aunty Amara, coming up behind Aunty Rosa and putting her arms around her. 'They'll be here. And if not, we'll all just make instruments out of the crockery and dance to that. It'll be fun!'

Aunty Rosa smiles at Aunty Amara. Aunty Amara is very good at calming Aunty Rosa down. She's her clay pot.

'Have you got my notes?' Aunty Rosa asks her. 'For my speech?'

Aunty Amara giggles. Aunty Amara is less good at remembering Aunty Rosa's notes. Or anything else for that matter. She once spent two hours looking for her car keys. And then another four hours looking for her car.

'Oooops,' Aunty Amara giggles again. 'Never mind, sweetheart. You don't need notes. Speak from your heart. I'm going to make up a poem about you on the spot. It'll be beautiful.'

All the adults pull a bit of a face.

Aunty Amara's last poem from her heart was on Granny's seventieth birthday, when she couldn't think of any rhymes for Granny's actual real name, Nancy. So the poem went something like:

Nancy, oh, Nancy ...
You smell like a French Fancy.

Fortunately Granny found it very funny and didn't get formidable about it at all, so that was good.

'If I may have your attention,' Reverend Wright announces. 'I would like to propose a toast to the happy couple.'

William U comes and stands next to me, holding Mr Nibbles to his ear, as if Mr Nibbles is talking to him.

'What's that, Mr Nibbles?' William U says. 'You're glad you didn't have to go home with stinky old Scarlett because … what's that? Oh, right … she smells worse than your cage before it's been cleaned …'

'Go away, William,' I say, feeling the angry bubbling up inside me.

'Yes, you're right – she is a poo-poo bum-head.' William U grins and holds Mr Nibbles so tightly, our poor class hamster is starting to squeal.

'Don't do that!' I snap. 'You're squeezing him.'

'Ladies and gentlemen,' Reverend Wright begins, 'it is my absolute pleasure to welcome you here this evening to celebrate the beautiful love between Rosa and Amara. I first met Rosa when …'

'Stop it!' I hiss at William U again as Mr Nibbles squeaks. 'You're hurting him!'

'I don't care,' says William U, not letting Mr Nibbles go. 'My mum says if anything happens to

Mr Nibbles, we'll just buy another stupid hamster and no one at St Lidwina's will know the difference.'

This is an awful thing to say. The angry bubbles are getting bigger.

'Everyone in Rainbow Class will know! Give him to me – NOW!' I say more loudly than I mean to, making the people nearest me turn around. Mum looks over from the other side of the room and gives me the be-quiet-the-grown-ups-are-talking look. William U just smiles back at her and starts to talk out of the side of his mouth.

'I don't care,' he says. 'I don't care about Rainbow Class. I don't care about Mr Nibbles. I just didn't want you to have him. And now you don't.'

He gives Mr Nibbles another little squeeze, making our hamster squeal again. I have to save Mr Nibbles.

'William U! Give him to me!' I demand, and lots of people turn around this time.

'Make me,' says William, still smiling at my mum, who is giving me Bad Looks. Uh-oh. She can hear. Mums can always hear when you're doing something they don't like. It's one of the things they learn at Mum School, along with how to cure everything, magic kisses, some Maths (*my mum must have been ill the day they did long division, by the way*) and talking for hours even when they say it's time to go home.

I reach for Mr Nibbles, but William U moves him out of the way. I try again, but I am too slow again. An idea hits me. If I am too slow to get Mr Nibbles out of William U's hand, perhaps I need William U to let Mr Nibbles go himself. I start to tickle William U's side.

'Don't!' he screams, squirming around. 'I'm allergic to tickling …!'

But I'm not going to stop – I am going to save Mr Nibbles. And it's working. A few tickles later and William U yelps, opening his hand and releasing Mr Nibbles. I try to grab him, but Mr Nibbles is too fast and scuttles off around the feet of the party guests. I can't see him. But I can see my mum making her way towards us.

'You idiot!' hisses William U. 'What did you do that for?'

'You were hurting him,' I tell William U, crouching down to look between everyone's shoes.

'Where is he?'

'Don't know, don't care,' sulks William U. 'Stupid hamster …'

'I can't see him,' I say, just as Mum comes over.

'What's all this noise?' she whispers not very quietly. 'What's going on?'

'Scarlett wants Mr Nibbles, but he's mine, so she lost her temper and hit me, so I dropped him,' William U gasps, looking as if he's about to cry.

'Scarlett, is this true?' Mum asks as William U's mum comes over, realising that Something Is Upsetting William.

'My William!' she gasps, grabbing him to her. 'You're … upset! What's Upset William?'

'Scarlett,' sniffs William, giving me an evil grin when neither mum is looking.

But I don't have time to worry about William U. I am too worried about Mr Nibbles. What if he's lost? What if someone accidentally steps on him?

What if he …?

'And that is the joy of love,' Reverend Wright declares with a smile. 'It lifts everyone. It lifts us all highEEEEEE! EE! EEEEE! AAAAAAHHH! AAAAAHHHHH! OOOOOOOOOOH!'

What if … what if Mr Nibbles has gone up the vicar's trousers?

'Reverend, are you OK?' Aunty Rosa asks as the vicar starts to dance around.

'Wow – an expressive dance about the beauty of love!' Aunty Amara cries, throwing off her shoes and joining in with the vicar's jerky movements.

'THERE'S SOMETHING IN MY TROUSERS!' the vicar screeches. 'I NEED TO GET IT OUT!'

'The Gents is just over there,' whispers Jakub, pointing the vicar towards the toilet, 'if you need to "pay a little visit …".'

But the vicar is now completely out of control as Mr Nibbles tries to find his way out.

'Yes, Reverend, yes!' cries Aunty Amara, spinning around like a carousel. 'I can feel something joyful dancing around your heart!'

'WELL, I CAN FEEL SOMETHING FURRY RUNNING AROUND MY TROUSERS!' screams the vicar, making one of the party guests choke on a chicken vol-au-vent. Reverend Wright knocks into waiters and vases, and tips over the whole buffet table, before Mr Nibbles escapes from his left trouser leg. I dive to the ground and pick our class hamster up.

'It's OK, Mr Nibbles,' I reassure him. 'You're not in any trouble. It's all going to be OK.'

I stroke him gently until he stops shaking. I get to my feet. My best party dress is covered in trifle and bits of quiche, but I wipe them down with something hanging up next to me. That's better. No one's going to notice a few crumbs on my dress. Or that lady's coat.

But as I stand up, I see a room full of shocked adults staring at me, with William U grinning smugly in his mum's arms.

'SCARLETT!' Mum shrieks.

Gulp.

Mr Nibbles might be OK.

But I am in big, big trouble.

ChapTeR 5 –2

I have never been in so much trouble ever, not even the time I pushed Emek over in the sandpit in Year 2 because he did a wee on my sandcastle.

'I CAN'T BELIEVE HOW YOU BEHAVED!' roared Mum in the car on the way home. 'You've embarrassed yourself, you've embarrassed me and you've TOTALLY RUINED your aunties' engagement party!'

One of the reasons I like Maths is because it always makes sense. But Mum's Maths doesn't always add up. Up until Mr Nibbles got up the vicar's trousers, she had been perfectly happy drinking Bubbly Mummy Juice for two hours, so I don't understand how:

2 hours x Having Fun

+ Drinking Bubbly Mummy Juice

+

2 minutes x Bit Embarrassed

+ Hamster in the Vicar's Trousers

=

TOTALLY RUINED!'

'What do you have to say for yourself?' Mum shrieked.

'It wasn't my fault,' I said. Because it wasn't. It was stupid William U's.

Mum did that thing a volcano does before it erupts, sucking in loads of air.

'NOT YOUR FAULT?! NOT YOUR FAULT?! SCARLETT FIFE, IT IS *ENTIRELY* YOUR FAULT!'

'Emi, love,' Jakub said quietly. (*Jakub hates it when I'm in trouble, by the way. After Mum sent me* to my room for the Emek thing, he sat outside my bedroom and sang me songs to stop me crying. Jakub is awesome.) 'Perhaps you should Just Calm Down.'

It turns out that 'Just Calm Down' doesn't work on mums either. Mum looked as if she might need to take her tights home in a Special Bag like Milly did.

'DON'T YOU DARE TELL ME TO "JUST CALM DOWN"!' she raged, not calming down even one little bit. 'Scarlett Fife, there will be Consequences for this ...'

And she meant it. It's now Monday and here are just some of the things I'm not allowed Until Further Notice (which is ages away, by the way):

⭐ Any screen time WHATSOEVER (at first I thought that meant I couldn't even look at the satnav, so had my eyes shut in the car until Mum told me that was OK).

35

✹ Anything with sugar in it *(including sugar)*.

✹ Sleepovers.

✹ Any discussion of ever having a pet *(bye-bye, Chunky the UniBunny)*.

✹ Fun *(or that's how it feels)*.

But the scariest one was left for last.

'I'm fed up with your temper spoiling our special occasions,' Mum warned. 'You spoiled last Christmas when you lost your temper over a cracker toy ...'

'What was I supposed to do with a set of mini screwdrivers?'

'You spoiled my birthday when you lost your temper over the ice cream ...'

'If it calls itself banana ice cream, it should taste like an actual banana!'

'And now you have spoiled your aunts' engagement party by losing your temper over a silly hamster ...'

'But I didn't!' I insisted. 'And he's not a silly hamster. He's Mr Nibbles and William U was hurting him …'

'You were in a bad mood about it before the party and I could hear you trying to take that hamster from the other side of the room!' she screeched.

'But … but …'

'No buts!' Mum shouted, pointing her finger to make it louder. 'Enough is enough, Scarlett! If you have ONE MORE temper tantrum between now and Aunty Rosa's wedding, I'm … I'm … I'm cancelling our trip to Super Mega Awesome Sicky Fun World!'

NOOOOOOOO!

This was Very Bad News. Mum booked the holiday to Super Mega Awesome Sicky Fun World because we were supposed to go on an aeroplane holiday to Greece, but Mum said we couldn't after Jakub lost his job. I really hope Jakub finds his job again soon as I really want to go on an aeroplane. Peter in Year 4 who collects stuffed octopuses went on one last summer and said you get your own TV. It must be a bit squashed if everyone has a widescreen on their lap, but I still really want to go.

Anyway, Mum booked the trip to Super Mega Awesome Sicky Fun World for the day after Aunty Rosa and Aunty Amara's wedding as a Special Treat. Super Mega Awesome Sicky Fun World is THE BEST theme park in the world – Jakub showed me a video of the Guts-a-Churno coaster and we've been measuring me every day to make sure I'm 135 cm so I can go on it. On October sixteenth, I was EXACTLY 135 cm, but now it doesn't matter if I'm a million centimetres because Mum *actually* sees her punishments (Mumishments) through. She has:

✻ *Actually* Turned This Car Around when I was five and we were supposed to go on a picnic and

I got angry about not putting on my alphabet song CD.

✻ *Actually* took Maisie home on a sleepover last year when we wouldn't go to sleep.

✻ *Actually* stopped a birthday party and sent everyone home for making bad choices (*that was Jakub's party, by the way – he gets Mumishments too*).

'I'm going to talk to your teachers too,' Mum promised. 'And if they tell me you've lost your temper at school, I will cancel the trip. Do you understand me?'

I do. And now I'm sitting on the carpet in form time and getting Maisie's red-glasses perspective on it.

'You should see this as an opportunity,' she says. 'Your anger has got you into trouble a few times now.'

'Like when?' I ask, not even slightly angrily.

'Like when Fleur didn't invite you to her party and you got all cross at her and had to go on The Cloud?' Maisie says.

'I just pointed out that Fleur had come to all my parties and it wasn't fair ...' I remind her.

'In the middle of prayer-time in assembly,' Maisie points out. 'Then there was the time you shouted at Vashti in the playground and had to sit on The Thinking Bench ...'

'She left me out of a game of catch!'

'You'd just broken your collarbone,' Maisie says, wiping her red glasses. 'You couldn't lift your right arm ... I'm just saying – this is a chance for you to learn how to handle your temper.'

'I don't have a temper!' I sort of a little bit shout back.

'*Q E two*,' says Maisie wisely.

'What does that mean?' I ask.

'It's Latin,' Maisie explains, 'for "yes you do".'

Miss Hugg rings the Quiet Bells and we all sit on our carpet spots for Morning Time. Miss Hugg is the nicest teacher at St Lidwina's. I've had to wait until Year 5 to get her and I am SUPER happy to be in her class.

'Good morning, Rainbow Class,' says Miss Hugg, suddenly putting her hand to her mouth.

'Good morning, Miss Hugg. Good morning, everybody,' we all say, except for William U who says it in French because he's a big bogie-head show-off.

'Well now – I have three exciting pieces of news this morning,' says Miss Hugg, looking a bit pale. 'The first is that we have a new student joining us at St Lidwina's!'

(St Lidwina, by the way, is the patron saint of ice skaters. In assembly, Mr Pitunity said that they named our school after her to teach us to always get back up

when we fall. But when Jakub looked up St Lidwina on the internet, he found out that she fell over ice skating when she was fifteen and hurt herself so badly she spent the rest of her life in horrible pain and never ice skated again. Perhaps she should have come to our school.)

Miss Hugg points to the classroom door where a New Girl is standing holding hands with her mum. New Girls are super exciting and everyone wants to be their Special Friend. When Maisie joined the school, I had to fight Vashti and Parva to be her Special Friend. Vashti decided it wasn't individual if we both wanted to be Maisie's Special Friend and I had to give Parva my toffee yoghurt at lunchtime, but I won.

'This is Polly,' says Miss Hugg, encouraging Polly to come and stand at the front of the class. Polly holds her mum's hand tightly, but her mum gives her a kiss and gently pushes her towards Miss

Hugg. 'Welcome to our Rainbow Family.'

Polly stands at the front of the room while we all sing our welcome song, where we say welcome in lots of different languages (*which is a bit weird, by the way, because unless you speak Croatian, Farsi, Chinese and Urdu, you won't know what we're singing about for half the song*). Polly is very pretty and has a really nice bow in her hair. It might be worth a toffee yoghurt to be her Special Friend ...

'Polly and her mum have just moved to the area and I'm sure you'll make them both very welcome,' says Miss Hugg. 'And if we're really lucky, Polly's mum Rita has promised to show us the ambulance she drives. Won't that be exciting?'

The class gives a big 'oooooh'. Polly's mum drives an ambulance? I immediately give up on being Polly's Special Friend. It'd take too many toffee yoghurts.

Miss Hugg gives Polly a carpet space (*a ladybird,*

which is the best one, by the way – I got a worm and had *BIG FEELINGS* about it at the start of the year) then pulls a piece of paper out.

'Now as you know, it's time to start rehearsals for our Christmas Play,' she says. 'This year, the play is called *The Star That Saved Christmas!*'

Another 'oooooh' from the class. This sounds really good. Or at least better than last year …

Let me explain something:

St Lidwina's has had a lot of different head teachers over the past two years. This time last year, we had Mr Weed, who decided that having a Christmas Play might offend all the people who don't have Christmas in their religion. Mr Weed worried about offending people a lot (*he took the Gentlemen and Ladies signs off the teachers' toilets so they wouldn't be offended – but Mrs Take from Year 2 was quite offended when Mr Point from Year 6 walked in on her doing a wee, so she made Mr Weed put them back*), so instead of having a Christmas Play, we did a Seasonal Event called *The Non-Specific Festival That Could be Anytime!* and we all had to dress up as vegetables (*because meat might have offended people who didn't eat meat*).

It was really rubbish and afterwards the parents of all the people who don't celebrate Christmas in their religion like Sarah (*who is Jewish*) and Shaun (*who is Muslim*) and Luke (*who is Jedi*) said that they weren't at all offended by St Lidwina's having a Christmas Play, but all the parents agreed they were very offended by St Lidwina's having Mr Weed as head teacher, so could he please leave now.

Now we have an executive head teacher called Miss Pelling. At first I got a bit confused, as I thought 'executive' was something to do with 'executioner', who is someone who chops people's heads off. But actually now I think 'executive' means 'not here very much' as I haven't actually ever seen Miss Pelling,

45

which is probably a good thing if she's just going to go around chopping people's heads off.

'Now I've thought very carefully about who should play which part,' says Miss Hugg. 'I want you to remember that all the parts are very important and I don't want anyone getting upset or boasting, OK?'

We all nod as if we believe her, but everyone knows there are good parts and rubbish parts. I was an artichoke in *The Non-Specific Festival That Could Be Anytime!* which I had VERY BIG FEELINGS about. It's my turn for a good part this year. I want to be the Star That Saved Christmas.

'Polly,' says Miss Hugg with a smile. 'Your mummy tells me you did lots of drama at your last school?'

'Yes,' says Polly quietly. 'And I go to Stage Starz on Saturdays.'

A group of kids gasp. There aren't enough toffee

46

yoghurts in the school to be Polly's Special Friend now.

'Wonderful!' says Miss Hugg. 'So that's why I've made you … the Star That Saved Christmas!'

WHAT????!!!!! This girl has only just walked in and she gets the best part?! That's not fair! I bet Polly has never had to dress up as an artichoke at Stage Starz …

'Now everyone else will be different Christmas traditions from around the world. William U, you will be Father Christmas,' Miss Hugg continues, looking nervously at William U's mum, who is looking nervously at Her William. But a big smile suggests that this has Not Upset William, so they both breathe a sigh of relief.

'Felix and William D, you are going to be the Yule Lads, the mischievous elves from Iceland!' Miss Hugg announces.

'Can I be a velociraptor?' asks William D, who

always dresses as a dinosaur for every dress-up day, World Book Day and even Victorian Day because he said they discovered fossils then so it counts.

'Maybe next time, William,' says Miss Hugg with a smile.

'Azuri, you are going to be the evil Krampus from Austria,' says Miss Hugg, putting a picture of a scary monster on the board. 'He punishes naughty children on Christmas Eve.'

'He sounds like my Uncle Brian,' says Azuri. 'He makes us listen to his awful guitar-playing every Christmas Eve ...'

I wait as Miss Hugg reads down the rest of the list revealing what everyone is going to be – Maisie is a shepherd for the third year in a row.

'I don't mind,' she says. 'Saves anyone having to get a new costume for me. Last year's tea towel probably still fits.'

Those red glasses are really good.

I wait and wait for my name, which Miss Hugg finally announces.

'And then Scarlett,' she smiles. 'You are going to be …'

I wait to hear my brilliant role. Maybe a fairy? Maybe a snowflake? Maybe …?

'… the Swedish Yule Goat!'

I did not see that coming.

'A goat?' I ask as William U bursts out laughing.

'Not just any goat – the Swedish Yule Goat!' says Miss Hugg, as if that makes it any better. 'In Sweden, they build a giant straw goat, thirteen metres high! Although sadly, people keep trying to burn him down …'

I don't blame them.

I don't care how high the Swedish Yule Goat is. I want to be the Star That Saved Christmas. I have **BIG FEELINGS**. I can feel the angry bubbles in my tummy.

'At least the Swedish Yule Goat is tall enough to go on the Guts-a-Churno coaster,' Maisie whispers, but I don't really want her red-glasses perspective right now.

Miss Hugg smiles at me.

'You'll get to sing a special song and everything! It's a wonderful part, Scarlett. Just like they all are,' Miss Hugg adds quickly, shooting a look at Freddie who's going to be a deep-fried caterpillar from South Africa.

I can feel my angry getting bubblier in my tummy. This is rubbish! I want a good part in the play! But I have to keep my temper in. If I go on The Cloud, I can kiss the Guts-a-Churno coaster goodbye ...

'Muuuuum!' William U wails, looking up at his mum.

'I think What's Upset William is that he'd like to sing the special song,' whispers William U's mum. 'Perhaps Scarlett could let My William sing her song …'

'I … er … um …' Miss Hugg flusters, looking as if she's going to throw up.

'The casting is final,' a firm voice booms from the back of the room.

We all turn around to see a gigantic lady standing in the doorway.

Azuri puts his hand up.

'Is that the evil Krampus?' he asks.

'You're early,' says Miss Hugg to the lady. 'I was just—'

'I'm perfectly on time,' says the lady. 'You are running late.'

'Yes … my fault,' says Miss Hugg. 'Do come in

… Now, children, the third piece of exciting news is … well, it's to do with me, really … you see, I'm having a baby!'

Rainbow Class go wild. A baby is SUPER exciting.

'I want a baby!' William U moans.

'Mummy will talk to Daddy,' William U's mum promises.

'However,' says Miss Hugg, shaking the Quiet Bells, 'the baby is making me a little … queasy. There's nothing wrong – the baby and I are really well. But until the baby is here, I'm going to have to stay at home.'

NOOOOOOO! Miss Hugg is the best teacher in school – I've waited ages to have her! By the time she gets back from having her silly baby, I'll be in Year 15 – babies take ages. My angry starts to bubble up again.

'But don't worry, I'm leaving you with a wonderful

teacher,' says Miss Hugg nervously. 'Children, let's give a special Rainbow Class welcome ... to Ms Pitt-Bull!'

We sing our welcome song again as Ms Pitt-Bull comes to the front of the class.

She is wearing PE kit and carrying a big flask of green sludge. I've heard of Ms Pitt-Bull – she covered for Mr Peters in Year 6 when he had to go and think about his choices after the PTA Spring Social. Sasha in Year 6 said Ms Pitt-Bull used to be a prison warden in an American prison called Alcatraz. She is super strict. This is not good.

'Thank you, children,' says Ms Pitt-Bull without smiling. 'I look forward to getting to know you all.'

'You're a stupid goooaaaat, you're a stupid goooaaaat,' I can hear William U chanting behind me. The **BIG FEELINGS** are getting really bubbly now.

'Thank you, Miss Hugg,' says Ms Pitt-Bull, standing in front of her. 'Now first things first. I need some parent helpers for our class trip to the wildlife park. You are to ask your parents if they can come with us on Thursday.'

'I'm happy to come,' says Polly's mum, who is still standing at the back of the class.

'My dad will come,' I say suddenly, although I haven't actually asked him.

'Good,' says Ms Pitt-Bull. 'Please ask him to confirm with me in an email this evening.'

'I bet your dad won't come,' William U whispers. 'My mum comes to everything because I'm the best in Rainbow Class. And you're a stupid gooooaaaat ...'

I refuse to turn around. Stupid William stupid U isn't going to cost me my trip to Super Mega Awesome Sicky Fun World. But I can feel the angry bubbling up inside me. I focus on Ms Pitt-Bull's flask of green sludge to take my mind off William U. But the more I look at it, the more it is starting to ... fizz. Whatever's in there is really gross. My bet is broccoli.

'Rehearsals for the play will start tomorrow,' says Ms Pitt-Bull, handing out the scripts. 'Please learn your lines as soon as possible.'

'You won't have any lines,' whispers William U. 'Because you're a stupid goooaaaat …'

I bite my lip and keep on looking at the flask. It is really fizzing now, so much so it is starting to rock.

Now William U is making goat noises behind me. I'm still looking at Ms Pitt-Bull's smoothie. I am getting angrier and angrier and angrier. It's not fair that I'm a stupid goooaaaat, it's not fair that Polly is the Star That Saved Christmas, it's not fair that Miss Hugg is leaving us with Ms Pitt-Bull, it's not fair that …

Oh no. I close my eyes and squeeze my fists. I don't think I can hold it all inside – it feels as if I'm going to explo—

SPLAAAAAAAAAT!!!

I open my eyes. What's happened? Everyone sitting near the front is covered in a thin

layer of green goo ... I look at the flask.
The top has flown off and the green slimy
contents have exploded all over the classroom.

This is too much for poor Miss Hugg, who grabs
the recycling bin and does a very big sick in it, just
like the one Mum says she'll probably do when she
goes on the Guts-a-Churno coaster.

I look around the classroom, which is now in
green slimy chaos. My hands are shaking. What
have I done?

'Scarlett?' I hear Maisie say. 'Scarlett, are you
OK?'

I look at her, still trembling.

'Maisie?' I say quietly. 'I think I just made that
smoothie explode.'

CHAPTER 2 X 2

Things My Dad Is Really Good At

1. Working from home, so he can pick me up after school every day.

2. Tickly kisses with his tickly beard.

3. Having one arm. He was born with one and he says it's the only one he needs. He sometimes uses another arm called a 'prosthetic' arm (*by the way, this is NOT the same as a 'Prosecco' arm, like I thought it was when I was four, which is apparently something different and lots of grown-ups have one*), but he doesn't always like or need it, so we mainly use it for hide and seek.

4. Making the BEST dippy egg and soldiers

(*when he doesn't burn the toast*).

5. Drawing and making stuff (*because he's a graphic designer, by the way*).

'So how was school?' Dad asks, putting my egg and soldiers down in front of me. (*By the way, adults often ask this question, but really the only answer they want is 'good'. If you say, 'Fine,' they'll say, 'Only fine? Why's that?' If you say, 'Bad,' then they'll say, 'I'm sure it can't have been that bad.' So if you want to do important stuff like watch TV, you need to say, 'Good.'*)

'Good,' I tell him. I don't think he'll understand about exploding smoothies and, anyway, I'm sure it won't happen again. 'Oh – I said you'd come and help on the school trip to the wildlife park on Thursday.'

'Oh, sweetie,' Dad says in that way that means he doesn't think I am sweet or like a sweetie at all. 'I'm really busy at the moment – it's hard running your own business ...'

'But you never come on school trips,' I sulk. 'Elizabeth's dad came to the miniature village AND the historic dockyard AND he runs his own business AND he has to go away a lot ...'

'Sweetie, Elizabeth's dad's … business … involved stealing things. He's had to go away for a few months to think about his choices.'

That's weird. Elizabeth says her dad has been sent on a special trip by Her Majesty. Although this would explain what happened in the miniature village gift shop …

'Anyway, please will you come?'

I give him the big eyes and the wobbly lip. This never works on Mum. She says she's 'immune' to it, which means she had an injection to stop it, like I did with tetanus and got a sticker for being brave. But Dad must have missed the injection, because it works on him **EVERY** time.

'OK,' he sighs. 'I'll email your teacher. Which other parents are going?'

'William U's mum …'

'Of course …'

'I think Felix's dads …'

63

'Do I know them?'

'Yes. They're the ones who came back to get you when you fell over in the dads' race on sports day. Do you remember? They won the race by, like, miles, and you pulled your hamstring just after you started and they had a drink, got their medals, then came back and carried you in their arms just like you were a baby and—'

'Who else?' Dad asks quickly.

'Oh. Polly's mum,' I grumble.

'Polly?' asks Dad. 'I've not heard you talk about her.'

'She's new,' I say, dipping a soldier and making an egg volcano. 'She's got the best part in *The Star That Saved Christmas*!'

'Oh yes, the

Christmas Play!' says Dad. 'What part did you get?'

I feel the bubbly anger again.

'The Swedish Yule Goat.'

'Brilliant!' laughs Dad, who makes all my costumes for the school plays because he's a graphic designer. 'That'll be fun. Better than the artichoke.'

'I wanted to be the star,' I grumble. Dad comes and gives me a big hug.

'You're always a star,' he says, giving me a big tickly kiss with his beard and making the angry bubbles go away. 'Now would you like some more toasty soldiers?'

I nod as I've nearly run out.

'How's Sandra?' I ask him. 'Is she coming round this week?'

'Ah,' he says, pulling an icky face. 'We broke up.'

Now this isn't exactly unusual. Miss Hugg always says that we shouldn't say someone is bad at something, there's a nicer way of putting it. So …

Things My Dad Finds a Challenge

1. Any sport that involves throwing or catching. (*By the way, he says it's not because he has one arm and that if he had two, he'd just be twice as bad.*)

2. Mashed potato (*ALWAYS lumpy*).

3. Dancing (*like all dads*).

4. DIY. (*Although he thinks he's really good. Like all dads.*)

5. Girlfriends.

Last year, my dad bought a toaster off the internet. But when it arrived it looked nothing like the picture and didn't do what it said it would. Dad learned an important lesson about toasters that day.

But he didn't learn the same lesson about girlfriends.

Dad spends a lot of time on dating websites that promise you'll find love. I don't know if he's using them wrong (*that was part of the problem with the toaster, by the way, especially after he did some DIY on it*), but he's not even finding girlfriends that he likes very much.

Just this year, there's been:

❈ Brianna, who juiced everything (*even bacon*).

BRIANNA
JUICE FOR LIFE

❈ Shakira, who had a nice profile picture (*which said she was thirty-two, when she was actually sixty-two – and it was of her sister*).

SHAKIRA
AGE 32 (REALLY!)

❈ Olga, who only spoke Lithuanian (*although she was actually thirty-two*).

OLGA
SPEAKS ENGLISH GOOD

❈ Tracey, who wouldn't go on a second date (*because Dad's carpet had bad energy*).

TRACEY
FLOWER POWER

And most recently:

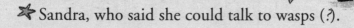

✳ Sandra, who said she could talk to wasps (?).

'What happened?' I ask Dad.

He shrugs. 'You'll have to ask the wasps.'

'You're really nice, you'll find someone,' I tell him. 'Someone who really likes you.'

'And my carpet,' Dad sighs. 'Do you know what, Scarlett? I'm done with dating. I've got you, I've got my business – that's enough for me.'

'You always say that,' I tell him. He always says that.

'Well, this time, I really mean it,' he insists. 'I, Bruce Fife, am single and happy. No more dating for me.'

The toaster pops up some burnt toast.

I hope that Dad has better luck with girlfriends than he has with toasters.

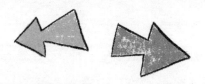

CHAPTER 10÷2

When Dad drops me back to Mum's, Aunty Rosa is sitting at our kitchen table with Jakub. Aunty Rosa is spending a lot of time at our house because she's helping Jakub after his boss, Gary, gave him the sack. At first, I thought Gary had given Jakub 'a sack', so didn't understand why this was a problem because Jakub cleans offices for his job and I thought a sack would be quite useful. But getting 'the sack' means he'd lost his job, which has absolutely nothing to do with actual sacks and this is why I don't like words as much as numbers.

Jakub told Aunty Rosa that he thought he'd got the wrong sort of sack because Gary doesn't like people who come from different countries. (*Which is just silly, by the way – there's a map at school that shows we have people from nineteen different countries at our school and I like all of them. Except for Alex, but that's not because of where he comes from, it's because he wipes his bogies on the back of your jumper.*) Aunty Rosa said that wasn't allowed and that Gary can't take Jakub's job away, whether he gives him 'a sack' or 'the sack'. So now Aunty Rosa is taking Gary to a court (*one where they don't play tennis*), where a judge can make Gary give Jakub his job back or some money to say sorry. I'm not sure what happens about the sacks.

But Jakub's (*not tennis*) court case is making everyone very stressed (*except for Aunty Rosa, by the way, who is always stressed anyway, so I don't think she minds*) because my mum is having to work lots of extra hours at her job to Make Ends Meet. My mum works as an engineer and makes buildings, so Making Ends Meet is very important otherwise her buildings would fall down. But Making Ends Meet is making her tired and grumpy and forgetful and there are a lot more Mumishments these days.

'Hey, squidge,' says Aunty Rosa, who doesn't seem nearly as cross about her engagement party as Mum keeps telling me she is. 'How's the hamster?'

'Rosa, please don't,' sighs Mum.

'*Rosa, please don't,*' Aunty Rosa mimics. Mum looks at her as if she does mind about her Big Posh House and earning more money after all.

Mum turns around. Oh no. She's wearing an apron. Mum is cooking …

Let me explain something:

Some mums are very good at cooking, but they'd Find Making Buildings a Challenge. My mum makes really good buildings, but she *really* Finds Cooking a Challenge. Miss Hugg says it's great to try to overcome Things We Find a Challenge. But then Miss Hugg has never eaten my mum's cooking.

Some of my mum's recipes include:

⭐Toast Chicken (*because it's so crunchy*).

⭐Forgetti Bolognese (*because she forgets to cook it properly*).

⭐Shepherd's Die (*because it tastes like one did*).

I look in the oven and can already see smoke coming out of it. Tonight, it's Blackeroni Cheese.

'So the hearing is scheduled for next Wednesday,' Rosa tells Jakub, 'and they will expect you to—'

'Can I watch TV?' I ask.

'Sure,' says Jakub, getting up to switch it on.

'No!' says Mum, snatching the remote away. 'No screens. You're still on Mumishments.'

'Oh, lighten up, Emi,' says Rosa. 'Rev Wright

was fine about the hamster. He said Mr Nibbles was nothing compared to the time he was doing a funeral and the body came back to life …'

'That's not the point,' says Mum firmly. 'Scarlett needs to accept the consequences of her actions. No screens.'

Rosa and Jakub go quiet. There is no point in arguing with Mum. It is like arguing with one of her buildings. One where the ends meet.

'So about the hearing,' Aunty Rosa continues, 'you'll need to bring—'

'Mum, have you done the invites for my party yet?' I ask her. It's my birthday next week and I am having the BEST party at Stuff-a-Squishie. Everyone LOVES Stuff-a-Squishie because you get to make a teddy (*I've already chosen mine, by the way, which is the new UniMingo – everyone loves UniMingoes because they're a cross between a unicorn and a flamingo and they're the actual best thing EVER*), then you get to pay extra to give it everything it needs, like clothes and a smell and a musical instrument and sports accessories and medical equipment and identity documents and stationery. I have been **SUPER** excited about my Stuff-a-Squishie party for ages and I am getting A LOT of toffee yoghurts from everyone who wants to be invited.

'Scarlett!' says Mum in a way that makes me think she hasn't done the invitations. 'We're busy right now, but we need to talk about your party …'

'Talk about what?' I ask. 'Talk about when you're going to do the invitations?'

'No,' says Mum, looking at Jakub. She does a big sigh. Big sighs are never good. 'There aren't going to be any invitations. I'm sorry, Scarlett – we just can't afford a Stuff-a-Squishie party right now …'

NOOOOOOOOOOOOOOOOOO!

I feel as if someone has taken my batteries out.

This can't be right? No Stuff-a-Squishie party? No UniMingo in lederhosen that smells like bubble gum with a ukulele, paraglider, stethoscope, National Insurance card and a lever-arch folder? But it's my—

'You're still going to have a party, though,' Mum says with a not-happy smile.

'Where?' I ask suspiciously.

'Mr Blister's Soft Play!' says Mum, trying to look happy. 'You love Mr Blister's!'

'When I was seven and a quarter!' I say, feeling the angry bubbles rise up. 'Now I'm nine and fifty weeks and two days! I'm too old for Mr Blister's – it's for babies! I don't want a party at Mr Blister's! I want a party at Stuff-a-Squishie!'

'Emi, perhaps I could—?' Aunty Rosa starts.

'NO!' shouts my mum. 'Scarlett, don't be so spoiled. I'm not paying Silly Money for a party!'

(*By the way, I know that in Europe they spend*

euros and in America they spend dollars. I don't know where they spend Silly Money, but since Jakub got the wrong sort of sack, my mum refuses to spend it. So now we don't go to the Posh Supermarket with the advert where they pour chocolate sauce on everything and give you a toy if you spend over £20 of Silly Money, we go to BargainMart where everything is called a funny name and they take normal money and don't give you a toy unless you pay for it.)

Mum takes a breath.

'Scarlett. We're all having to Make Ends Meet …'

'Well, I want to Make the Ends of My New UniMingo Meet!' I say, trying not to shout. 'You promised!'

'Well, things have changed!' Mum actually shouts. 'We can't all have what we want! So you're just going to have to—'

The smoke alarm goes off. The Blackeroni Cheese must be done.

'This isn't fair!' I try not to yell, the angry bubbles now squeezing out of my eyes, although that might also be because of the smoke from the Blackeroni Cheese. 'I just want my Stuff-a-Squishie party ...'

'Scarlett!' says Mum, slamming the smouldering Blackeroni Cheese down on the table. 'I've told you, you are going to have a party – at Mr Blister's! And if you don't stop being so spoiled, I will cancel that one too!'

'Calm down, Emi,' says Jakub. 'She's just disappointed—'

'DON'T TELL ME TO CALM DOWN!' shouts Mum, who might need a Special Bag in a minute. 'I'm working double shifts to pay the bills, we have no idea how this court case is going to go, I'm tired, I'm stressed and now I've burned the macaroni cheese!'

I can feel the anger bubbling up. This isn't fair. It's not my fault that Jakub got the wrong sort of

sack and that Mum has to Make Ends Meet and that the Blackeroni Cheese looks disgusting and it's sizzling away and making the kitchen smell and …

My angry bubbles up and bubbles up. I want to shout at Mum to tell her how unfair this is and how I've had a rubbish day too and how I'm a Swedish Yule Goat, I still haven't got Mr Nibbles, I'm stuck with Ms Pitt-Bull for the rest of the year and Polly is the Star That Saved Christmas.

But then I see the tickets for Super Mega Awesome Sicky Fun World pinned up on the Important Things Board. I clamp my mouth shut so the angry can't come out. It isn't fair that Jakub lost his job. It isn't fair that I can't have my party. And it really isn't fair that I have to eat Blackeroni Cheese, which is still sizzling and squelching like a troll's toilet and now it's spitting bits of cheese sauce all over the table. The bubbles inside me are getting bigger and bigger, so I squeeze my eyes shut so that the angry can't get out of them, because I just feel like any second I'm completely going to—

BOOOOOOOOOM!

I open my eyes.

'What was that?' Jakub shouts, taking his hands off his head and looking at the empty smouldering pot in the middle of the table. It's no longer full of Blackeroni Cheese.

But the kitchen is.

The Blackeroni Cheese has gone everywhere – all over the walls, all over the ceiling, all over Aunty Rosa's neat notes.

'Emi, look what you've done!' Aunty Rosa shouts, trying to wipe cheese sauce off her paperwork.

'I didn't do anything!' Mum shouts. 'It's Jakub's

fault – how many times have I asked you to clean that oven? It's full of burned food …'

'Well, whose fault is that?' Jakub says, getting as close to shouting as he ever does. 'You don't cook food, you cremate it! If you weren't so stubborn and let me do the cooking …'

I walk slowly out of the room as the adults start to argue in the kitchen. It's happened again. I've made something explode.

And I have no idea how to stop it.

ChapTeR 2 x 3

The day of any school trip should be super exciting because school trips are **THE BEST THING** you can do at school. You get a special lunch and you go on a coach AND you get to spend no-more-than-three-pounds-in-a-clearly-labelled-plastic-bag at the gift shop on important educational things like sparkly pencils.

But even though today is the day of the school trip, I'm not super excited. I'm super worried.

'I'm telling you,' I tell Maisie on the coach. 'I can make things explode.'

'I don't think you can,' says Maisie calmly. 'It probably just feels that way.'

'But I can!' I tell her again, feeling the bubbly

anger in my tummy again. 'Just this week, I've exploded Ms Pitt-Bull's smoothie, my mum's Blackeroni Cheese and an underwater volcano in Peru. I saw it on the news.'

A big giggle goes up from the back seat of the bus, where Polly is sitting in the middle of a group of girls. Not only is Polly the Star That Saved Christmas AND has a mum who drives an ambulance, but in the few days she's been at school, **EVERYBODY** wants to be her Special Friend. So many girls wanted to sit next to her for the wildlife park trip, she started a ticket system, just like the cheese counter at BargainMart. It makes my angry bubble.

'Fleur, it's Misha's turn now,' Polly says, making a grumpy Fleur move to the end of the row and a squealy Misha move up next to her. I'm not at all happy to see Fleur sulk at the end of the row, even though she didn't invite me to her party. Honest.

'Urgh – she's so … Polly,' I grumble to Maisie.

Maisie shrugs. 'She seems nice.' Maisie is my Bestest Forever Friend and I really like the fact that she's so kind and nice. It's just really irritating when I want her to complain about someone.

'I sat next to her in Golden Time yesterday and she showed me how to make friendship bracelets,' Maisie says, holding out a bracelet made out of knots on her wrist which would be really pretty except I hate it more than anything I've ever seen ever.

I can feel the bubbly anger bubble up some more.

'But we've already got friendship bracelets,' I remind her. 'We made them out of curly pasta last month.'

'Oh, those,' says Maisie quietly. 'My foster mum's dog ate them over half-term. We can make some more if you like?'

'No, it's fine,' I say grumpily, obviously meaning that it isn't fine at all.

'Oh, OK then,' says Maisie. Maisie means everything she says and assumes that everyone else does. It's a very strange way to behave.

'Anyway,' I say, as another giggle bomb goes off at the back of the bus, 'this exploding thing – what am I going to do?'

'Scarlett,' says Maisie, which she always does before she tells me something I don't want to hear. 'Do you remember the time you thought you gave Freddie chicken pox?'

'I might have done,' I reply.

'Even though you've never had it?' Maisie says, as if that has anything to do with it. 'Or the time you decided that you started a tsunami in Malaysia because you did a botty pop in PE?'

'It was a big botty pop,' I remind her.

'And now you think you can explode things,' says Maisie. 'Do you think there's a chance you're wrong about this too?'

This is a matter for probability. Probability is when you figure out how likely something is to happen – so if you flip a coin there's a one in two (or fifty per cent) chance of it being head or tails. If you roll a die, there's a one in six (or … something per cent) chance of rolling a six. I quickly figure out the probability of me being wrong.

Probability of me being wrong = 0 per cent
Probability of me being right = 100 per cent

'No,' I say now I've finished my calculations. 'You have to believe me. I *am* making things explode.'

'If you say so,' says Maisie, looking out of the window. 'If you say so,' is Maisie-speak for, 'I know I'm right and you're wrong, but I don't want to upset you so I'll just say, "If you say so."'

I hear my dad laugh and look up to the front of the coach where he has taken his Prosecco arm off

85

and is passing it around the bus. There are lots of gasps of 'cool' and 'awesome', mainly from Polly's mum Rita who is sitting next to him. My dad is very kind like that, always making people happy.

William U is at the front of the coach too, because his mum says he is allergic to coaches and has to sit at the front. This means that Rory, who is *always* sick on school trips, is sitting further back in the coach and has had his green head buried in a paper bag the whole trip.

The coach stops outside the wildlife park and Ms Pitt-Bull stands up.

'Right, Rainbow Class,' she booms. 'Please remember that you are ambassadors for our school, so I expect your very best behaviour and want to see lots of our Priority Values. What does that mean?'

I put my hand up. (*I know all the Priority Values, by the way, because part of being an executive head means that even though Miss Pelling's not there, she's* taken down displays called 'Believe in Yourself!' and 'Let's Treat Everyone With Respect!' and replaced them with posters about 'Growth Mindset' and 'Priority Values', which basically mean we should believe in ourselves and treat everyone with respect.)

'Freddie?' Ms Pitt-Bull asks.

'I need a poo,' Freddie announces. Freddie always needs a poo. Miss Hugg tried to encourage him to keep it private, so made him his own special passport (his 'poosport'), which he could show her when he needed a poo. Freddie must have left it in his tray. The poosport, not the poo. Although there was that time ... Actually Miss Hugg said we weren't to tell that story as it's Freddie's Private Business.

'We will have a toilet stop before we take our tour,' Ms Pitt-Bull answers. 'But back to our Priority Values ...'

'This poo is becoming a Priority Value ...' says

the squirming Freddie as Rory does a big sick in his bag. Ms Pitt-Bull has a lot to learn about Freddie. A lot of teachers learn a lot about Freddie, usually with a mop and bucket.

'William D?' says Ms Pitt-Bull, upsetting William U who thinks his waving hand is going to be answered.

'Will there be any dinosaurs?' William D asks.

'No, William,' says Ms Pitt-Bull. 'Dinosaurs have been extinct for millions of years. The wildlife park is full of living creatures. But back to our Priority Values ... Polly?'

'Respect, Manners and Good Listening,' says Polly.

'Excellent, Polly,' says Ms Pitt-Bull. 'Three Positivity Points.'

THREE POSITIVITY POINTS??? For saying something everyone knows??? That's like giving Freddie three Positivity Points for having a poo ...

'Right, everyone,' says Ms Pitt-Bull, clapping her hands. 'Collect your lunch on the way past, find your partner and line up outside the bus.'

Actually, I am a bit excited. School packed lunches are really nice. (*So long as you don't get the egg sandwiches. What is the point of egg sandwiches, by the way? No one likes egg sandwiches and the only people who do like egg sandwiches, no one likes them.)* I already know what I'm getting because I told my mum to order it on the special form: cheese sandwiches, salty crisps, a toffee yoghurt and ginger biscuits. I can't wait.

'Scarlett Fife ...' says Ms Pitt-Bull, checking her list as I go past. 'I didn't receive a form for you.'

'But I told my mum ...' I begin. I remember the form on the Important Things Board ... and now I think about it, it was still there last night. Mum must have forgotten to hand it in. Mum is forgetting everything at the moment. I feel the bubbly anger start to bubble.

'Well, I'm telling you, I haven't had it,' Ms Pitt-Bull says, still looking at her list and grabbing a bag. 'So the dinner ladies just had to guess what you wanted ...'

She hands me a brown paper bag. I don't have to open it to know what is inside. You can smell it from the middle of next week …

'But I hate egg sandwiches,' I moan.

'Think of all the children living in poverty around the world who don't have enough to eat,' says Maisie. 'They'd eat your egg sandwiches.'

'Well, they can have them,' I snap. 'I want cheese—'

'Scarlett,' Ms Pitt-Bull says sharply. 'I had an email from your mother about your temper. I hope you're going to keep it under control.'

Brilliant. So Mum could remember to email Ms Pitt-Bull about my temper, but not about my cheese sandwiches. I can feel the angry boiling up inside me. But I mustn't get cross with Ms Pitt-Bull. Not only will I lose my trip to Super Mega Awesome Sicky Fun World, but Sasha in Year 6 says that Ms Pitt-Bull used to be the prime minister's bodyguard and knows judo and karate and Kung Pao, so you shouldn't mess with her.

'Here you go,' says a voice behind me, holding out a bag. 'I'll swap with you. I like egg sandwiches.'

I turn around to see who this cheese sandwich angel is …

It's Polly.

'Polly, that's very kind of you,' says Ms Pitt-Bull. 'Five Positivity Points for thoughtfulness.'

FIVE??? I can feel Mr Nibbles getting away from me again. Polly's going to get Mr Nibbles. Just like she got the best part in the play. And the back seat of the bus. And now my egg sandwich, even though I don't want it, but that's not the point. I take her bag quickly in a way that isn't snatching at all.

'Scarlett?' says Ms Pitt-Bull sharply. 'What do you say?'

'Thank you,' I say, a bit like when the dinner ladies put broccoli on my plate.

'You're welcome,' says Polly, skipping back to her

friends. What a show-off ...

I walk away just as William U's mum starts telling Ms Pitt-Bull all about Her William's Sandwich Aversion Syndrome and why he can only have chocolate cake and cheesy puffs in his lunch box that she made specially.

'Did you see that?' I say to Maisie as we line up. 'Can you believe Polly?'

'She did a really nice thing,' says Maisie.

'She just wants Mr Nibbles,' I inform her. I know I'm right, because I am.

'So do you,' says Maisie. 'You're both being super good to get Mr Nibbles. *Squids go pro* ...'

'What ...?'

'It's Latin for "doing something to get what you want",' says Maisie. 'That's why you cleaned the canteen after lunch. That's why you ate broccoli.'

'That was different,' I point out, the anger bubbling away harder now.

'If you say so …' says Maisie, as Freddie shoots past us holding his bottom and Rory does another big sick in a bin shaped like a hippo.

I get in line to go into the wildlife park as

everyone squabbles over who is going to be Polly's partner.

Cheese sandwiches or no cheese sandwiches, this is officially the **WORST** school trip ever.

ChapTeR 2 + 3 + 2

This is the **BEST** school trip **EVER**!

We are in a special room where we have been given a talk about the animals at the wildlife park and how they've been rescued from the wild where they aren't able to take care of themselves, which reminds me a bit of when Mum asked Jakub to come and live with us. Now we've got a chance to meet some of the animals and stroke them if we are very gentle. I get to stroke a guinea pig and a lamb and a monkey (*who, by the way, scratches his bum, which also reminds me of Jakub*).

Now we get to go out into the wildlife park with our parent helpers to see the animals.

'Mrs Foster?' Ms Pitt-Bull asks Polly's mum.

'Please, call me Rita,' says Polly's mum, waving to the class. Everyone waves back, but I think that's because she drives an ambulance.

'Rita,' asks Ms Pitt-Bull. 'Are you happy to take a group of children around the wildlife park?'

'Of course.' Rita smiles as Polly goes to hold her hand.

'Excellent,' says Ms Pitt-Bull. 'You'll need another parent helper to go with you ...'

'I'll go!' says my dad, shooting his hand up like William U in a Name the Syndrome competition.

'Is that OK?' Ms Pitt-Bull asks Rita.

'That would be great,' says Rita, smiling again and looking at my dad, who smiles back.

Although he didn't want to come, Dad looks as if he's having a really good time now we're at the wildlife park. He's in such a good mood, he is even being super kind to Polly's mum, always making sure he holds doors open and stays with her everywhere and laughs at all her jokes. My dad is very kind like that.

But it does mean that Maisie and I have been put in a group with Polly and her partner Milly (*being Polly's partner at the wildlife park had cost Milly all her toffee yoghurts for a month, by the way*), as well as William D and his partner Karam. Karam only came to our school this year, because he had to leave his country as there's a Big War there. We had an assembly about it and we all felt very sad for Karam and very grateful that we live in a country that doesn't have a Big War.

Karam doesn't speak very much English, so he has Fatima to help him translate from Arabic. But he does play really good football, and luckily football plays the same in Arabic as it does in English. He also really likes dinosaurs, so he and William D spend a lot of time together learning how to say dinosaur names in each other's languages. It's really fun having Karam in our group because he can teach us the Arabic for everything we see.

We go and see a giraffe (*zirafa*), lions (*'aswad*) and tigers (*alnumur*). But my favourite is Ellie, the big African elephant (*fil*). Ellie has been rescued from hunters who wanted to hurt her with their guns. But more importantly, she can produce up to 130 kg of poo (*biraz*) every day.

'She must need a really big poosport,' says Freddie, coming up with his group, which Ms Pitt-Bull is looking after.

'Who can tell me what you call a group of elephants?' Ms Pitt-Bull asks.

We all put our hands up.

'Polly?' Ms Pitt-Bull asks.

'A herd,' says Polly, making Milly burst out in a round of applause.

'Well done,' says Ms Pitt-Bull. 'Three Positivity Points.'

Another **THREE** Positivity Points???!! At this rate, Mr Nibbles is going to move in with Polly. I am **GOING** to get the next question right, no matter what.

'Who can tell me …?' Ms Pitt-Bull asks. I shoot my hand up in the air to make sure I'm first. 'What is the name for the head of the herd?'

Argh! I heard Polly's mum read this off the sign in the enclosure, but Ellie was doing a really big wee (*bul*). Loads of other people have their hands up now. She probably won't pick me anyway …

'Scarlett?' Ms Pitt-Bull asks.

Rats. I'm thinking so hard my brain itches, but I can't remember what Rita said. Miss Hugg says there is no such thing as a silly answer and that we should always try. So I'm going to have a go. What would be a good name for the head of an elephant herd? Something majestic. Something important. Something like …

'Dave?' I answer.

Everyone starts laughing. Apparently there is such a thing as a silly answer.

Dad is laughing. Rita is laughing. Even Ms Pitt-Bull is laughing and she probably only laughs at 9.34 at night when everyone is asleep and she thinks no one is watching.

'It's "a matriarch", Scarlett,' says Ms Pitt-Bull. 'But I think we'll put your answer in the Memory Jar.'

I can feel the bubbly anger rising up as everyone laughs at me. So Polly gets three more Positivity Points and I get to go in the Memory Jar where only silly things go, like when Felix asked if mature Cheddar was more sensible than the other cheeses and when Alex got a pencil lead stuck in his ear. I am NEVER going to get Mr Nibbles. I try to squash down the angry bubbles.

A bleeper goes off and Polly's mum raises her hand.

'I'm so sorry Ms Pitt-Bull, I've just been paged,' says Polly's mum. 'There's been a big accident and

I've been called into work. I'm going to have to get a taxi back.'

'Of course,' says Ms Pitt-Bull, as everyone mutters again about how cool Polly's mum is. At least they're not still laughing about Dave.

'I'll come with you – we'll split the cost,' says Dad quickly. 'If that's OK with you, Ms Pitt-Bull.'

'Absolutely,' she says. 'It's nearly home time anyway – we'll be fine.'

'Is that all right, Scarlett?' Dad asks me, still looking at Polly's mum.

'OK,' I say, obviously wanting him to stay. This is my school trip and he never comes. He can at least stay until the end.

'Great!' He grins and heads off with Rita, chatting away as they rush through the wildlife park. The angry bubbles are getting bigger.

'Scarlett, are you OK?' Maisie asks, noticing me clenching my fists.

'It's happening again,' I tell her.

'OK, just breathe ...' Maisie says.

'I'm getting cross, not having a baby!' I snap at her. 'Just leave me alone ...'

I obviously don't mean that. But Maisie thinks I do and goes quiet.

'Right,' says Ms Pitt-Bull as all the other groups join us. 'It's time to go to the gift shop.'

The bubbles evaporate immediately. Learning about animals and conservation and stuff is really important.

But the gift shop has sparkly flamingo pencils.

'Line up with your partners and I will give you your bags,' Ms Pitt-Bull instructs.

Everyone races to get in line. I want to be near the front to get my no-more-than-three-pounds-in-a-clearly-labelled-plastic-bag, but Maisie is never in a rush for anything, so we end up right at the back.

'Are you feeling better?' Maisie asks quietly as the

line moves towards Ms Pitt-Bull.

'Maybe,' I say, a bit embarrassed about how grumpy I've been. 'What are you going to get at the shop?'

I've worked out exactly what I'm going to buy and done the sums to make sure they add up, even

£1.59
£0.78
£60.00
£62.38!

making the decimal points all line up because when I didn't the sum went wrong and it was going to cost me £62.38 which is more than I got for Christmas and my birthday put together. I'm going to get:

A sparkly flamingo pencil	=	£1.59
A candy cane	=	£0.79
A monkey rubber	=	£0.60
TOTAL	=	£2.98

(And that gives me two pence change, by the way, which means it's good value for money.)

'I think I'm going to put my money in the donation bucket,' says Maisie, who always does stuff like that. It might be her red glasses or it might be because Maisie Finds Maths a Challenge, which is why she's on the Orange Table for Maths because she doesn't know her nine times table quite yet.

'It says that three pounds will feed a long-eared rabbit for a day,' Maisie says.

'That's nice,' I say, thinking about all the things I can do with my sparkly flamingo pencil.

We move up the line, Ms Pitt-Bull giving everyone their no-more-than-three-pounds-in-a-clearly-labelled-plastic-bag. William U is in front of us, where Ms Pitt-Bull is taking the clearly-much-more-than-three-pounds out of his clearly-labelled-plastic-bag.

'Oh, the thing is,' William U's mum whispers to Ms Pitt-Bull, 'My William needs a bit more than the other children. He has Gift Shop Dependency Syndrome. We don't want William to Get Upset ...'

'Everyone has the same,' says Ms Pitt-Bull, returning the extra money to William U's mum. 'Next!'

Maisie and I are next.

'Here you go, Maisie,' says Ms Pitt-Bull, giving her a plastic bag. 'And Scarlett ... I don't appear to have one for you.'

'What?' I say.

'Pardon?' says Ms Pitt-Bull sternly.

'**WHAT?**' I say more loudly so she definitely hears it this time, feeling the bubbles start up again in my stomach. Ms Pitt-Bull raises an eyebrow.

'I'm sorry, Scarlett,' she says. 'Your parents don't appear to have supplied you with the money for the gift shop.'

'But-but-but …' I stammer. I can't believe it! First the egg sandwich, now this! I know Mum is very busy Making Ends Meet, but what is the point of earning money if she isn't going to give it to me for a sparkly flamingo pencil?

'I'm sorry,' says Ms Pitt-Bull. 'But I cannot give you what I do not have. Perhaps your parents didn't want you to have the money?'

'But they did!' I say, the bubbles coming up so hard now, they are squeezing water into my eyes.

'It's OK, Scarlett – you can have my gift shop money,' says Maisie.

'No!' I almost shout. 'If I take your money then the long-eared rabbits will be hungry, just like the children living in poverty around the world who only get old egg sandwiches! I just want my money!'

'Scarlett,' says Ms Pitt-Bull in a warning tone. 'Remember your temper. You don't want to go on The Cloud …'

I squeeze and squeeze to keep the anger inside. Ellie the Elephant has just done another big poo and I try to focus my eyes on that to stop me from getting angry.

'Right,' says Ms Pitt-Bull. 'Remember to meet me by the gift shop exit in ten minutes.'

I feel the anger bubble and bubble. There is no point in going to the gift shop. I can't get my sparkly flamingo pencil. I can feel the cheese sandwich in my stomach starting to churn.

'Scarlett?' whispers Maisie. 'Are you OK?

You look really … weird.'

But I can't answer her. I know that if I open my mouth, all the angry is going to come out. I'm angry about my sandwich, I'm angry my dad left my trip, I'm super angry about my sparkly flamingo pencil, but if Ms Pitt-Bull hears, I'll go on The Cloud and I can kiss goodbye to Super Mega Awesome Sicky Fun World. So I close my eyes and squeeze super hard before I—

KERSPLAAAAATTTTTT!

I hear a yelp, a big POP and then a large, wet SPLAT. I open my eyes.

The big pile of elephant poo is no longer there.

But standing on the other side of the enclosure, frozen to the spot, is William U's mum.

And she is covered in exploded elephant poo.

'Woah,' whispers Maisie, standing next to me with her jaw on the floor as William U drops his souvenirs worth definitely-more-than-three-pounds-whether-you-had-a-clearly-labelled-plastic-bag-or-not. 'You were right. You *can* make things explode.'

I watch as William U's mum wipes the poo from her eyes and William U starts to wail about being allergic to elephant poo.

I am glad that Maisie believes me. But that doesn't

solve my problem. Yes, I can make things explode.

But I still have no idea how to stop it.

Chapter 2 x 2 x 2

Let me explain something:

If you need help with your hearing, you are given a hearing aid to help you, like my grandad was when he was still alive (*he also had false teeth that he used to put in his water, by the way, until his friend Edna accidentally drunk from his glass and then he and Granny weren't allowed to go to her Golden Wedding Party*). Most grown-ups don't need a hearing aid. But they could really use a listening aid. My mum says that your body goes through lots of changes as you grow up and she'll explain them to me when I'm a bit older, so I expect to hear all about the listening problem.

When grown-ups get really old (*like thirty*) their

listening ears just don't seem to work any more. This problem is particularly bad for parents. Parents can listen to politics, a message on their phone and someone talking about that mum at the school gate who is having lots of extra tennis lessons. But they just don't listen to their children any more. Like when it's someone else's fault, or when you're trying to explain how that new game works or why a pet is **SUPER** important.

But the good news is that once parents aren't able to listen to their children (*or each other*) any more, they can pay other people to do it for them. And that is my Aunty Amara's job.

Aunty Amara listens to anyone who might be worried or sad or upset about something and she helps them to find creative ways to feel better. If there were a gold medal for the best listener in the whole wide world, she'd win it – and she'd know exactly where to go to collect the prize because she would have listened very carefully to the instructions (*unlike Petra, by the way, who ALWAYS talks in assembly, so Rainbow Class is never first to leave the hall*).

So I am very happy Aunty Amara picked me up from school today. I'm still very worried about making things explode – what if it happens at her wedding and I ruin the whole day? That would mean I lose my trip to Super Mega Awesome Sicky Fun World. I need help. And if anyone can help me, it is Aunty Amara.

'Aunty Amara,' I ask her on the way home. 'Do you ever talk to children who are really angry?'

'All the time,' says Aunty Amara. 'Anger is often our way of telling someone that we're really unhappy about something. It's like a red stop sign, showing people we've had enough. It's a very useful emotion.'

That's interesting. I've never thought of anger as being useful before.

It just seems to get me into trouble.

'And when these children get angry, does anything ... happen?' I ask her.

Aunty Amara stops and looks at me with a big, kind smile.

'Why do you ask?' she says. 'Are you angry about something?'

'No,' I say so quickly it means I must be telling the truth. 'It's for my friend ... Cara. She gets very angry.'

Aunty Amara smiles again. She clearly has no idea I'm talking about myself.

'I see,' says Aunty Amara. 'So what is ... Cara's ... problem?'

'Well ... she's finding that when she gets angry, things ... I mean ... for example ... things ... are sort of ... exploding?' I say carefully. I don't want to give too much away. I'm very good at that.

'That makes sense,' she says, nodding. 'Anger is

a very explosive emotion.
That's why people can
shout or scream, or
even get physical
when they are
angry. All that
anger has to go
somewhere. It's
like slime in a
party bag. No
matter how much
someone tells you

to keep it in, it's always going to find its way out.'

'I see,' I say, feeling she's slightly missing the point I'm trying not to make. 'So ... if you tried not to get angry about something ...'

'Well, I think that's very hard,' Aunty Amara says. 'You're either angry or you're not. Once you're angry, you need to find a healthy way of getting it out. Otherwise it might come out in ways you don't want it to.'

A light bulb goes on over my head. It's that new street lamp that Mr Morgan at number 54 wrote to the council about – but I also realise something important. This must be it! Because I am trying to keep my anger in, it is making other things explode! That makes perfect sense. But if I let my anger out in the wrong way, I might not be able to go to Super Mega Awesome Sicky Fun World. So I need to find a way to let it out without getting into trouble.

It really is like slime in a party bag.

'So what's a healthy way to get anger out?' I ask. I'm worried this involves broccoli.

'Well, there are lots,' says Aunty Amara as we arrive at my house. 'Let's sit outside.'

'Sure,' I say, as we both sit on the swings in my front garden.

'So this friend of yours …?'

'Lara,' I remind her. Aunty Amara really does have the worst memory.

'Lara. Where does she feel this anger?'

'In her tummy,' I say truthfully. 'She told me.'

Aunty Amara smiles. 'It sounds as if you're being a very good friend to Lara.'

'Zara,' I correct her.

'Of course.' Aunty Amara nods. 'So when ... Zara finds herself getting angry, one of the most important things to do is to breathe.'

'I don't think she stops breathing,' I say. 'I think I would have noticed that.'

'But this is a special kind of breathing,' Aunty Amara explains. 'Breathing is like ... a remote control for our bodies and brains. It can tell them what to do. When you are angry, breathing tells our brains to calm our bodies down. Tell your friend to try this ...'

She holds up all ten of her fingers.

'Imagine these are birthday candles,' says Aunty Amara. 'Now try to blow each one out as slowly as you can.'

I try it. I'm not feeling the bubbly angry **BIG FEELINGS** right now. But by the time I finish blowing out my own fingers, I do have Big Giggles. So does Aunty Amara.

'You see – we both feel better already,' she says, starting to swing. 'Another important thing to understand is what's causing your anger. Anger can be the costume that other feelings are wearing. Sometimes it's easier to feel angry than to feel worried or embarrassed or disappointed. We call these feelings "triggers", like the thing that makes a gun go off.'

I think back to the explosions over the past few days and why I got so angry. The smoothie was because I was disappointed about the play. The Blackeroni Cheese was because I was upset about my party. And the elephant poo was because I couldn't have that sparkly pencil. They all just felt really unfair. Perhaps that's a trigger for me.

'Once you know your triggers, you can start doing something about them before it's too late,' Aunty Amara explains.

Aunty Amara makes a lot of sense. No wonder

people pay her to listen to their children.

'But the most important thing to understand is that, no matter how you try to manage it, you will get angry sometimes. And that's perfectly healthy and normal. We all get angry.'

'You don't,' I say.

'Oh yes I do!' laughs Aunty Amara. 'Just ask your Aunty Rosa. Some people have very BIG FEELINGS about us getting married. And I can get very angry about that, believe me ...'

I nod wisely. I overheard Mum saying to Jakub that some people weren't coming to the wedding because they had a phobia of homes. Phobias mean you're really scared of something, like Vishna has arachnophobia, which means she's really scared of spiders (*by the way, this isn't no-anorak-phobia, which was how I heard it in Year 3 and thought Vishna was really scared of losing her coat*). It must be very lonely having a phobia of homes – you can't go for playdates and make friends. How sad for anyone who can't do that.

'What do you do when you're angry?' I ask her.

'I remember all the good things and people in my life,' says Aunty Amara, swinging higher. 'And there are lots more of those than the bad ones.'

'Miss Hugg says that people aren't bad, they just Find Things a Challenge,' I tell her.

'Miss Hugg is a very wise lady,' Aunty Amara says with a smile. 'So I don't think too much about the people who Find Our Wedding a Challenge. And if I do, I just punch a cushion.'

I laugh. I can't imagine Aunty Amara punching anything. She is so calm, so wise, so clever.

'Hello, monkey,' says Jakub, jumping on my swing with me and starting to go really high. Jakub isn't like many grown-ups, but I think that's because he's quite young for one. He's eight years younger than my mum, which lots of people laughed about when they were first together, but I don't understand why. No one laughs when it's the other way around and the boy is older than the girl. Max and Serena in Sparrow Class are boyfriend and girlfriend and his birthday's in November and hers isn't until March – no one's laughed about that.

'What are you doing out here?' says Jakub, nearly flying over the top of the swing.

'We're just having a chinwag,' says Aunty Amara, trying to match his swinging.

'Well, you can wag your chins inside the house!' Jakub cries as we whoosh past on our swing.

'No, we can't!' squeals Aunty Amara, her beautiful dark hair flowing behind her as she kicks off her shoes and lies back on her swing. 'I've completely lost your house keys.'

ChapTeR 11 – 2

Today we are rehearsing for *The Star That Saved Christmas!* Even though Maisie is coming over for a playdate afterwards and we are going to have sausages and mash, which is our absolute favourite, I am not in a very good mood. We are in the school hall and Polly is on the stage doing her singing and dancing.

'Wow,' says Maisie. 'She's really good.'

'She's OK,' I say, shrugging and going back to making my glittery Christmas decoration. Actually, Polly is really, really good. But two people don't need to say it.

At the back of the hall is a massive Christmas tree and all of us have to make our own Christmas decoration for it, filled with glitter and something that is really important to us. Maisie is brilliant at drawing and she has made a really pretty heart because she says that love is important to everyone. I Find Drawing a Challenge, so Ms Pitt-Bull said that I could write a sum, as Maths was something that was important to me. I am writing my favourite sum (*8 x 8 = 64, by the way*) and putting it in my decoration.

'That's stupid,' says William U, coming up behind me with his Father Christmas hat on. 'No one puts a sum on a Christmas tree.'

I turn around to shout at him, but then I remember what Aunty Amara said and instead I take some deep breaths. I feel my body start to calm down and I only want to shout at William U a little bit. It's working …

'Actually somebody does put a sum on a Christmas tree,' I reply calmly, painting the second

126

eight. 'I do. So you are mistaken.'

(*Miss Hugg says we shouldn't say anyone is wrong, by the way. We should agree that they 'are mistaken' or 'we have a different point of view'.*)

'Well, I think it's stupid,' says William U.

'Well, I think we have a different point of view,' I say. I feel the anger starting to bubble, so I hold up my fingers and blow them like the birthday candles.

'What are you doing?' Maisie asks.

'Blowing the candles out,' I say back.

William U bursts out laughing.

'Ha!' he sneers nastily. 'I know your mum can't afford a Stuff-a-Squishie party because no one will give your stepdad a job, but now you don't have a real birthday cake either!'

Ouch. That hurt.

I can feel the bubbly anger getting much bubblier. I blow the candles harder.

'Go and have-a-different-point-of-view away,' I puff.

'William, you are being very unkind,' Maisie says calmly. 'I think you should go to the Thinking Bench and reflect on your choices.'

'*Well, I think you should go to the Bum Bench and reflect on your own bum,*' William U mimics.

'Sticks and stones …' sighs Maisie.

'Huh?' says William U. 'Speak English …'

'It *is* English. It's idiotomatic,' Maisie explains. 'And it means "if you keep speaking to us like that,

I'm going to tell Ms Pitt-Bull".'

'OOOOOOH, I'm so scared!' William U says, looking not very scared at all. 'My mum is a governor and she can get Ms Pitt-Bull fired and …'

'William,' comes a stern voice across the hall. 'I didn't quite catch that?'

William goes very pale. He turns around to face Ms Pitt-Bull. He's right to be scared. Sasha in Year 6 says that Ms Pitt-Bull was a fighter pilot in World War 4 and she takes no prisoners. (*I didn't think there had been a World War 4, by the way, but Sasha in Year 6 says that it's like* Home Alone 4 *– just because you haven't heard of it, doesn't mean it doesn't exist.*)

Out of nowhere, William U's mum speeds over and puts her arm around her son.

'My William!' she wobbles. 'What's Upset William?'

She looks accusingly at me and Maisie.

129

'I just heard William say my name,' says Ms Pitt-Bull, coming over. 'Why don't you share your views with us all, William?'

William looks like Freddie does when he's lost his poosport. It makes me feel better and the bubbly anger is going away.

'I … er … I was just saying that m-my mum is a governor and she w-was so happy that Ms Pitt-Bull w-was hired,' he stutters.

'Oh, William,' says his mum, giving him a cuddle as if he's just saved a dying puppy. 'What a lovely thing to say.'

Ms Pitt-Bull's eyes go very long and pointy. William U is frozen to the spot.

'It's time for your song, William,' she says. 'I suggest you leave Scarlett and Maisie to their jobs and you go and do yours.'

'Yes, Ms Pitt-Bull,' says William U, as he scuttles to the stage looking like Mr Nibbles on his wheel.

'Well done,' says Maisie. 'You handled that really well.'

'Thanks,' I say, smiling. It feels really good. Perhaps I can control this thing after all?

My dad and Polly's mum Rita laugh over the other side of the hall. Polly's mum volunteered to paint some scenery. Dad is really good at drawing and painting, so he offered to help too and then they had lunch to decide what to draw and paint. My dad is very helpful like that.

'Hey, I'm super excited about our playdate tonight,' I say to Maisie. 'I'm afraid we can't watch TV as I'm still on this stupid screen ban. But I thought we could do glitter stickers, then slime-making, then the spray stencils, then the pottery wheel, so that should keep my mum happy. Then we can …'

I look over at Maisie who now looks as if she's lost her poosport.

'Scarlett … I'm really sorry,' she says in a wobbly way.

'Sorry about what?' I ask, my tummy starting to bubble.

'The playdate,' Maisie says. 'My foster mum left a few messages for your mum, but she never heard back. So she made … different arrangements.'

My angry bubbles hard.

'What kind of … different arrangements?' I ask, starting to blow the candles out on my hand.

'A … different … playdate … arrangement …' says Maisie, quickly putting her heart inside her decoration.

'Who?' I ask, blowing so hard a bit of spit comes out.

Maisie puts down her pencil and tries to hold my hand.

'It's Polly,' she says quietly. 'My foster mum met Rita when one of my foster sisters got a pen lid stuck up her nose and they got talking – it was nothing to do with me ...'

The bubbly anger is bubbling super hard. Rita laughs again. As if she's laughing at me.

'But ... we've got sausage and mash,' I say, now blowing so much that my fingers are getting really wet and spitty. 'And Dad's cooking, so it's not going to be Mum's Squashage and Bash ...'

'Polly's got sausage and mash too,' Maisie says quietly.

The bubbles start to burst in my tummy.

'So you like her sausage and mash better than mine?' I say quite loudly.

'No ... I don't know ... I haven't tried her sausage and mash,' says Maisie, looking as if she wants to cry. 'And I'm sure it's not better. Just ... different. Scarlett, you're still my best forever friend – this means nothing – cross my heart, never lie, stick a sausage in my eye ...'

'Don't you talk to me about sausages!' I hiss at her, throwing my pencil back in the pot. It's too late. The bubbles are looking for any way out. Ms Pitt-Bull is glancing over at us, so I have to keep them in or I'll be sent to The Cloud and can kiss goodbye to the Guts-a-Churno coaster.

I am so angry. Angry at my mum for forgetting yet another Important Thing, angry at Maisie for having sausage and mash at someone else's house and angry with Polly for getting everything I want. Another huge laugh goes up between Dad and Rita. And there is my own dad, laughing away with Polly's mum. I am ready to burst.

I look at the big paint pot sitting between Rita and Dad. I try to breathe through the anger, but it is already too late. I watch as big bubbles start to form on the surface of the paint. As the bubbles grow in my tummy, the pot froths and spits like a pan of boiled eggs until the paint starts to spit out of the pot.

'Scarlett,' Maisie whispers. 'Scarlett, you have to calm down. Everyone will see …'

But the sound of Maisie's voice just makes me angrier. I shut my eyes and squeeze the anger down before it can come out of my mouth because I'm so full up of angry I just feel as if it's all going to …

SPLOOOOOOOOOOSSSSSHHHHH!

I hear a big wet splash, followed by a surprised squeal. I open one eye.

There, covered in purple paint, are Dad and Rita. For a moment, they just stand there in shock. I wait for them to scream, shout, use Bad Choice Words …

But instead, they just burst out laughing. And because they are laughing, all the people around them start laughing. And then the people next to them start laughing. Soon, the whole hall is full of people laughing.

'Phew,' Maisie says. Maisie and I are the only people not laughing. 'That was lucky. But, Scarlett, you've got to get this under control. Someone could get hurt. Or worse, you could lose your trip to Super Mega Awesome Sicky Fun World.'

I know that Maisie is right.

I just don't know what I am going to do about it.

CHAPTER 40 – 30

Today is my tenth birthday. Birthdays are the BESTEST thing ever because you get presents. If I put my presents on a bar graph, they'd look like this:

UniMingo calculator (big bar)

UniMingo water bottle (slightly less big bar)

UniMingo changey changey sequin jumper (really big massive bar)

UniMingo pencil case (really big bar)

Weird soap set from Great-Aunty Pat (not on the chart)

This morning I got breakfast in bed (*made by Jakub, by the way, so it was actually nice*), got to watch TV (*yes!*) and Granny and Aunty Rosa and Aunty Amara came round for lunch. It was really special to be with my family, because then I got even more presents.

Now it's time for my party. I had been super excited about my old party at Stuff-a-Squishie. But this new one at Mr Blister's Soft Play isn't nearly as exciting. Everyone has their birthday at Mr Blister's Soft Play and it's always the same. Everyone gets weird pink squash. Everyone gets pizza and chips. Everyone gets a verruca. It's sooooo boring.

'Come on, Scarlett,' says Mum in the car on the way there. 'Surely the most important thing is celebrating with your friends?'

'It is the most important thing,' I grump back. 'But the second, third and fourth most important things are UniMingoes with ukuleles and official documentation.'

'When I was little,' Jakub adds, reaching back and trying to tickle me, 'we didn't have Stuff-a-Squishie. My birthday party was a few friends coming around for cake. I loved it.'

'That's because you didn't have Stuff-a-Squishie,' I grump again.

I see Mum's face in the mirror. She has sad eyes. Now I feel bad. Angry eyes, disappointed eyes and I-expected-more-from-you eyes I can cope with. But sad eyes make me ... really sad.

'I'm sorry, Scarlett,' she says quietly. 'Maybe we can do Stuff-a-Squishie next year?'

'Thanks,' I say, trying to be less grumpy. Next year everyone will be into something else. But I don't say that because I'm trying to be less grumpy.

We pull up outside Mr Blister's Soft Play.

'Careful!' Mum says as Jakub gets out of the

car with the birthday cake that she's baked. That's another thing I'm trying not to be grumpy about. I'd wanted the UniMingo cake we'd seen in the Posh Supermarket, but Mum said she could make one without paying Silly Money for it. Mum has never made a birthday cake before, so I don't know if she Finds Birthday Cakes a Challenge. But I do know that she had to buy all the cakes she'd made for the bake sale to raise money for the wildlife park trip herself, so that's not a good sign.

My friends are already waiting inside. I've been allowed to invite five friends, which was really hard as I have lots more than five friends and I don't want to upset anyone like when I wasn't invited to Fleur's party, even though I'm totally fine about that now. So after a lot of thinking (*I got a lot of toffee yoghurts this week*), I chose Maisie (*before she became Polly's Special Friend, by the way*), Elizabeth, Tanika, Emma R (*who, by the way, is allergic to dairy*) and

Marcia (not Fleur – HA!). But as I get out of the car, there are six girls there. And only five of them are my friends.

'Polly?' I ask, as Dad joins us. My parents have a friendly divorce, not an angry divorce like Kevin's parents, who have to have separate parents' evening appointments. So that means all of my parents come to all of my parties and Christmases and stuff. I thought this was really good, until Kevin told me he gets two birthdays and two Christmases. Mum says that a friendly divorce is much better for me, although hearing about Kevin's two trampolines, I'm not sure how.

'Happy birthday, munchkin!' says Dad, picking me up and flying me around. 'I mentioned your party to Rita and invited Polly, so you two can get to know each other better.'

'Great,' I say, feeling the bubbles start to bubble up again. There were lots of people I wanted at my birthday party. Even Fleur would have been better than Polly.

'I hope you don't mind?' Rita says to my mum.

'Of course not,' says Mum, giving Dad the we'll-talk-about-this-later look. I might get two birthdays next year after all.

As Mum goes over to the manager to pay Silly Money for Polly to come to my party, Maisie comes quietly towards me.

'Hi,' she says, handing over a pretty present. We still haven't made up from our argument about her playdate with Polly.

'Hi,' I say, taking the present. It is very small. Mum says that when it comes to presents, it's the thought that counts.

But I still prefer big thoughts.

'Do you want to open it?' Maisie asks.

'Maybe,' I sulk, even though I really do.

Inside is a little velvet box. Good things often

come in little velvet boxes (*unless you're Fabien and his mum, by the way, because Fabien kept all his old scabs in a little velvet box he found at the back of a cupboard, without him or his mum realising it had an engagement ring inside it – at least until Fabien's mum's boyfriend proposed on Valentine's Day*).

I open up the box.

'Wow,' I gasp as I see what's inside. Sitting on a tiny pillow is a silver heart necklace with 'BFF' on the front.

'Look,' says Maisie, opening it up. It's a locket – and inside are two pictures, one of me and one of her.

It might be a small present. But it's a really big thought.

'You're my bestest forever friend,' says Maisie quietly.

'You're my bestest forever friend too,' I say back, smiling at her. 'Let's make up.'

We have a hug and say the make-up promise (*'make friends, make friends, never ever break friends, if you do, you'll be flushed down the loo and that will be the end of you*) so it's official.

'Come on,' she says, grabbing my hand. 'Last one in the ball pit gets an egg sandwich!'

'And a verruca!' I cry, running off with her.

We run into Mr Blister's soft play (*keeping our socks on, by the way*) and jump into the ball pit. Maybe because I haven't been there since I was seven and a quarter, I've forgotten how much fun it is – and because Maisie has never been at all, it is super fun to play with her for the first time. She thinks everything is exciting.

'Wow – there's a slide like a snake!' she shouts. 'Wow – let's climb up that net! Wow – there's a fully grown man stuck in that tunnel! Wow! Wow! Wow!'

After we've been running around for about five

hours (*Mum says it's been twenty-five minutes, but adults can't tell the time, by the way, which is why they need so many devices*), we really need some weird pink squash, so we sit down at a table for a drink.

'So,' I ask, pretending I don't care, 'how was your playdate with Polly?'

Maisie looks as if she doesn't really know what to say.

'It was … fine,' she says eventually.

'Just … fine?' I ask, sounding very casual. I'm very good at sounding very casual.

'Yes,' she says. 'Just fine. Although …'

'What?' I say quickly and incredibly casually.

'The sausage and mash wasn't as good,' she whispers. 'There weren't any lumps in the mashed potato. It was weird …'

I smile. Casually.

'If I say something, will you promise not to get cross?' Maisie asks quietly.

147

'OK,' I say, feeling cross bubbles starting to build in my tummy.

'I think you should get to know Polly,' says Maisie very quickly, as if she's trying to be casual or something. 'I think you two would be friends. You've got a lot in common.'

'Like what?' I ask, so casually it is almost invisible.

'Like ... you're both really good at Maths,' says Maisie. 'You both really like UniMingoes. You both have the same duvet cover ...'

'Really?' I say.

'Really,' says Maisie. 'And ...'

'And what?' I ask.

'And I really want to be friends with you both,' says Maisie. 'But if it's going to upset you, then you're my BFF and I'll never speak to her ever again, I swear, even if I need to ask something really important like if it's spaghetti for lunch.'

I look at my bestest forever friend in the whole

wide world and I feel the bubbles start to melt away. I'm not being very fair to Maisie. I think about what Aunty Amara said about my triggers and try to explain why Polly makes me so cross.

'Of course you can be friends with her,' I say quietly. 'It's just … it just feels like everything I want she's getting. Star of the Week, Mr Nibbles, the best part in the play …'

'How you doing, munchkin?' says Dad, running up all red-faced with Jakub and drinking the weird pink squash straight out of the jug. I think it's sweet how parents pretend that parties are for the children, when really it's just an excuse for them to run around at the soft play. Dad and Jakub were having an epic fight in the ball pit, but one of the People in Uniform had to ask them to stop as they were scaring the little children.

'This place is AWESOME,' says Jakub, stealing my squash. 'Brucie, race you to the snake slide?'

'You're on!' says Dad, running back into the play frame. I look over at Mum and Rita, who are rolling their eyes with a smile.

'Well, you've got something that Polly would give anything for,' Maisie says, looking over the top of her red glasses. I get ready for her different perspective.

'Like what?' I ask again. 'Polly has the best clothes, the coolest toys and she is the most popular girl in Rainbow Class. What could I possibly have that Polly wants?'

Maisie looks over at Dad and Jakub racing each other down the slide.

'A dad,' says Maisie quietly. 'Polly's dad died two years ago. That's why she moved to our school, to get a fresh start. She doesn't have a dad. And you've got two. I bet she'd swap Mr Nibbles, Star of the Week, the best part in the play and all her cool stuff to have her dad back.'

I look over at Polly, who is now on the slide with my dad. I had no idea. So she doesn't have her daddy any more? That's so sad. I don't need Maisie's red glasses to see this different perspective.

'I ... I didn't know,' I say, feeling really icky. There am I getting all upset about silly things like plays and playdates and Mr Nibbles, when Polly has had something so sad happen to her.

Although I still really want Mr Nibbles.

'*Happy birthday to you,*' I suddenly hear everyone sing. '*Happy birthday to you. Happy birthday, dear Scarlett ...*'

All my family and friends gather around as Mum brings over her cake, topped with ten candles. She puts it down on the table. It doesn't look anything like a UniMingo, unless the UniMingo was hit by a truck carrying glitter and sprinkles. But it does look like the best cake I have ever seen.

'Thanks, Mum,' I smile, as I blow out my awesome candles on my awesome cake surrounded by my awesome friends and awesome family. I smile at Polly and she smiles back. That feels better. Perhaps we can be friends.

But she'd better have got me a decent present.

ChApTeR 5 + 6

Today is an **INSET** day. (*This is not to be confused with an* **INSECT** *day, by the way, which is what I used to think it was in Year 1 and I thought all the teachers were spending the day with ladybirds.*) **INSET** day is when the teachers learn how to teach, which is a bit weird, because I really think they should know how to teach before they get a job in a school. (*Although that would explain how Mr Buss in Year 3 got his job even though he left two of his class at the leisure centre and brought back two children from Marshwold Community School because they wear blue jumpers too – I hope he learns a lot on* **INSET** *day.*)

But **INSET** days are super exciting because it means you get the day off school. Here is a pie chart of how I planned to spend my **INSET** day:

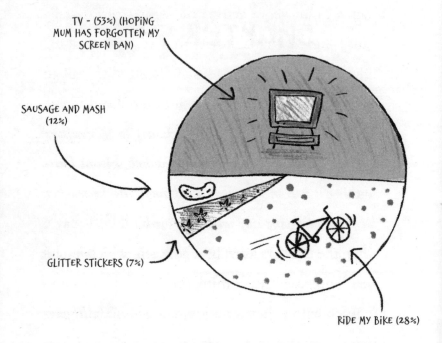

TV – (53%) (HOPING MUM HAS FORGOTTEN MY SCREEN BAN)

SAUSAGE AND MASH (12%)

GLITTER STICKERS (7%)

RIDE MY BIKE (28%)

But here is my mum's plan for **INSET** day:

Go to Jakub's Not Tennis Court Case (100%)

Today is also the day when Jakub goes to Not Tennis Court about getting the wrong sack. I really want Jakub to win because I love him and I want the judge to help him to find his job again so we can go back to having Pizza Fridays and not Board Game Fridays when Mum and Jakub argue over Monopoly.

But I also really want my day off school, so I asked Mum if I could stay with Dad.

'No,' said Mum.

That was the end of that conversation. I've had some bubbles in my tummy ever since.

So now we're in a court room (*which really does look nothing like a tennis court, by the way*) and Jakub is having to explain why he thinks it was unfair that he lost his job. His old boss, Gary, said he couldn't afford to keep him, but then hired someone else the next week. Aunty Rosa is arguing that Jakub lost his job because Gary doesn't like people from other countries, which makes me very bubbly because it

doesn't matter what country you're from. Cleaning is the same in every language (*boring*) and anyway Jakub is Polish and 'Polish' looks just like 'polish' (*even though they don't sound the same, silly words*), so even the word is good at cleaning.

Aunty Rosa has been asking Jakub lots of questions and he looks really, really nervous. He's wearing a suit, which doesn't suit him at all (*which is weird, because a 'suit' should 'suit' everyone*) and he keeps pulling at his collar as if it's hot, even though it's November. Aunty Rosa smiles at him (*which is super rare, so Jakub must have done really well*) and now the Other Lawyer who isn't Aunty Rosa is going to ask him questions too.

'Mr Nowak,' he begins, which is funny because I always forget Jakub has a grown-up name because I often forget Jakub is a grown-up. Jakub forgets it a lot too. 'Did you enjoy your job with Mr Biggs?'

'Yes,' says Jakub, looking as if he really

needs Freddie's poosport.

'And would you say you did a good job?' the Other Lawyer asks.

'Yes, I believe so,' says Jakub. I've never seen him look this serious for this long. I keep expecting him to stand on his head or make a farty noise. I wonder if I should make one to calm him down …

'You do, do you?' says the lawyer, which is silly, because Jakub just said he did and he needs to hurry up so I can get home and enjoy my INSECT day. 'Because according to this file, you had several absences from work … Where were you the week of September sixteenth for instance? It says here that you didn't come to work?'

'Ah – I had a … medical situation,' says Jakub, going bright red.

'I see,' says the Other Lawyer. 'Do you have any paperwork to prove this? A doctor's note? A hospital record?'

Jakub glances at Aunty Rosa, who looks stressed again.

'Er … no,' says Jakub, going bright red. 'It wasn't that kind of situation.'

'What kind of … situation was it?' asks the Other Lawyer in a way that makes me think he doesn't really care and is just trying to get Jakub into more trouble.

'I … I don't want to say …' Jakub whispers.

The Other Lawyer looks at the judge.

'Mr Nowak,' says the judge, 'it would be helpful for us all to understand why you missed a week of work.'

'OK …' says Jakub. 'Well, it started when I was climbing a tree with my stepdaughter, Scarlett …'

I stand up and wave at everyone so they know who I am, but Mum takes my hand and pulls me back down again.

'And we were having a competition to see who

could climb the highest,' Jakub continues.

Oh yes – I remember that day! We went to have a walk in the forest and Jakub and I climbed our favourite trees. But then …

'But then I fell out of the tree,' Jakub explains. 'And on to a log underneath. I didn't break anything, but I was very badly cut and bruised.'

'Cuts and bruises are a shame, Mr Nowak,' the Other Lawyer continues. 'But I fail to see why they should stop you doing your job. Where did you hurt yourself?'

Jakub looks really embarrassed.

'It was … it was … it was …'

'IT WAS HIS BUM!' I stand up and shout to the judge. 'He fell flat on his bum on the log and he couldn't walk and couldn't sit down without a rubber ring and Mum even had to help him when he needed to go for a …'

'Thank you, Scarlett,' Mum hisses, pulling me

back down again. I don't understand – I'm only trying to help. Miss Hugg says you should find a way to help someone every day – if she were here, I think she'd give me three Positivity Points for telling the Not Tennis Court about Jakub's sore bum.

'Er … I see …' says the Other Lawyer, looking all flustered and embarrassed as if he's never fallen out of a tree and hurt his bum so badly that he has to sit on an inflatable flamingo ring like Jakub did that week. 'Well, this doesn't explain the times you were late …'

'That was only one time,' says Jakub, starting to look cross. 'My car broke down.' (*Our car always breaks down, by the way, so Jakub is telling the whole truth and not the truth with holes in it.*)

'Or the complaints about your work …'

'There were NEVER any complaints about my work from anyone but Gary!' Jakub shouts. 'I worked so hard for him …'

I feel the bubbles rise up. Jakub really did work super hard at that job, cleaning offices every night and doing nice things like putting more water in the flowers and leaving little happy notes for people. The office people at the place he cleaned were so happy, they sent him a massive hamper last Christmas full of chocolates and biscuits and Bubbly Mummy Juice to say thank you. They wouldn't have done that if he wasn't very good at his job. This is so unfair …

Oh no. Unfair. Trigger …

'And then there's the matter of the missing money,' says the Other Lawyer, looking at the judge again.

'That was NOTHING TO DO WITH ME!' says Jakub, standing up and looking as if he could make an elephant poo explode.

'Objection!' Aunty Rosa shouts. 'My client was found completely innocent when that money was

found in someone's gym bag! It was a groundless allegation!'

I didn't know about this. Poor Jakub. It's bad enough being accused of stealing money you didn't take. But a ... groundless alligator? That must have been really scary. And very hard to clean.

'Sustained,' said the judge. 'The last comment is to be stricken from the record.'

'They're making a record of this?' I whisper to Mum.

'A record as in a document, not a record as in vinyl,' Mum whispers back. Silly words. But that makes more sense. Who'd want to play this record? My dad has some really weird records from the Victorian period in 1976 when everyone had long hair and silly trousers, but even he wouldn't want to play this one.

Jakub looks really sad. I'm feeling really angry. I look over at his boss, Gary, who is sitting smiling horribly. He's so mean. And he has silly hair – the top bit doesn't even match the bottom bit and he has something on his head that looks a bit like Mr Nibbles having a nap. I feel the bubbles rise up.

'The fact is, Mr Nowak, that there are too many examples of you failing to do your job,' the Other Lawyer says. 'I suggest that your dismissal has nothing to do with where you were born and everything to do with you not doing your job properly.'

Jakub goes to say something, but Aunty Rosa shakes her head to stop him. The bubbles are getting bigger. I look at Mum and I think she's really bubbly too. She holds my hand so tightly it's getting a bit pink. I know I mustn't shout as I could cause Jakub a lot of trouble. But this is so unfair and I'm so, so angry. I look at his horrible boss with his horrible hair, just grinning in his horrible way. The bubbles are getting bigger and bigger …

'I am going to adjourn,' says the judge. I've no

163

idea where that is and I don't see why the judge's holiday plans are important right now, but it doesn't matter because I'm trying so hard to keep my temper in. I start to blow out the candles.

'What are you doing?' Mum asks because I'm blowing quite loudly as I'm really cross.

'I will rule on the case next Friday,' says the judge, looking at his notes.

'Next (blow) Friday?' I say to Mum. 'That's (blow) the (blow) wedding (blow) day (blow).'

'It's OK,' says Mum through gritted teeth. 'The wedding isn't until the evening – there's time.'

I look at Gary shaking the Other Lawyer's hand. He looks as if he's won. I know that look – we get it every time we play Holy Trinity CE Primary School at football. They think that they're so much better than us just because they've got matching kit. And because they always score more goals. Just because Gary is a big meanie, it doesn't mean he's better than Jakub. The bubbles are getting huge – they have to go somewhere or I'm going to scream. I keep looking at Gary being congratulated by the people he's with, even though he's done nothing other than be mean to my Jakub and have horrible Mr Nibbles hair. I shut my eyes and try to stop the trigger from going off on my gun, but I think it might be a bit too late because I feel as if I'm going to …

BAAAAAAAAAAAM!

A gasp goes up around the Not Tennis Court and I know it's happened again.

As I open my eyes, Gary is standing very still. He looks very surprised.

And rather embarrassed.

And incredibly bald.

His Mr Nibbles hair has blown off his head. And as I turn to see where everyone is looking, I can see where it has landed …

Right on top of the judge.

Whoops.

Chapter 3 x 4

After the Not Tennis Court, Aunty Rosa offered to take us all out for lunch at the Posh Pizza Place because she's got more money than we have. Normally Mum says no because she's so all right with Aunty Rosa having a Big Posh House and more money than us that she doesn't need Aunty Rosa to pay for things, but today she just said yes. I like going out for lunch because you get colouring and ice cream and fizzy drinks – and today Mum says I can have those things even though I'm on Mumishments, which is super good.

But even that hasn't stopped me from feeling very worried – it's only a few days until Aunty Rosa and Aunty Amara's wedding and I'm still making things explode. What if it happens at the wedding? What if my temper explodes instead and I lose my trip to Super Mega Awesome Sicky Fun World? What if I have another slice of pizza while I think about it all?

Jakub was very upset after the Not Tennis Court, so he and Mum have gone for a walk to Cool Down, which makes sense because it's November. I'm trying to do a word search (*I'm stuck on 'tomato', by the way*) and Aunty Rosa is doing emails on her phone. But after today, I'm now super worried about the wedding. I look at Aunty Rosa muttering Bad Choice Words at her phone. Aunty Rosa's always getting angry. Perhaps she can help me?

'Aunty Rosa?' I ask her very casually.

'Yes, squidge,' she replies – to me, I think, not her emails.

'How do you stop yourself from getting angry?' I ask her, so casually I hardly even notice it.

Aunty Rosa puts her phone down and looks at me.

'I don't,' she says simply. I like talking to Aunty Rosa. She always has simple answers.

'Oh,' I say, going back to the word search to try to find 'tomato'. 'But … don't you get into trouble?'

'Sometimes,' smiles Aunty Rosa, winking at me. 'But there's some trouble that I like getting into.'

That wasn't such a simple answer. A bit like 'tomato' in this word search.

She leans over the table to hold my hand.

'Anger isn't always a bad thing,' she says. 'Sometimes it's only by people getting angry that things change for the better. Take the woman I'm named after – Rosa Parks. She got angry that Black people were treated so badly that they weren't even allowed to sit down on the bus if a white person wanted their seat. So one day, she sat there anyway. Her being angry started some very important conversations about civil rights.'

I think about that for a moment. So there is

a good angry? That's interesting. And helpful for getting a seat on the bus.

'And your mum is named after Emmeline Pankhurst,' Aunty Rosa says, 'a lady who got angry that women weren't being given the same rights as men. Her being angry meant that a whole movement started to campaign for women to have equality. History is full of people who have brought about real social change by getting angry.'

This is massive. So next time I get cross about Mum and Jakub not wanting to watch what I want on TV, I'm going to tell them that I'm 'bringing about real social change'. That should work really well.

'I have to get angry to do my job,' Aunty Rosa carries on. 'I get angry about the way that other people are treated, about things that are unfair and about how people try to get away with being unkind.'

'But how do you stop it becoming a problem?'

 170

I ask her. 'When I get angry, I just get in trouble.'

'Well, firstly, you have to choose what you get angry about,' smiles Aunty Rosa. 'There are things I get angry about that maybe I shouldn't. Those things I usually take out on kick-boxing.'

Aunty Rosa gets angry about a lot of things. She must kick a lot of boxes.

'But there are other things I *should* get angry about. And when that happens … well, I try to do something about it. That's what a lot of my job is about – doing something about the things that make me angry. If I do something about it, it makes me feel better.'

I sit back and look at

my word search. Suddenly I can see 'tomato' going diagonally backwards from the bottom corner. The answer was in front of me all along. I just couldn't see it.

It's just a shame that doesn't help me with not making things explode.

Mum and Jakub come back in looking much cooler.

'Hey, monkey,' says Jakub, picking me up and giving me one of his big hugs. 'Thanks for coming today. It was so good to see your beautiful face in that horrible place.'

I hadn't thought of that. I'd been so grumpy about missing my INSECT day, it hadn't occurred to me that it might make Jakub happier if I was there. That was a thing I shouldn't have got angry about. I'll kick a box later.

'Word search – cool!' says Jakub, sitting down next to me as Mum and Aunty Rosa have a big hug.

172

'Look – I've found "xkjfivub"!'

Jakub is so silly. He doesn't get very angry very often and not for very long, so perhaps it's a good thing that he's got people like Aunty Rosa to get angry for him. And perhaps I need to think about things that it's OK to be angry about and things that it's not. Like a table. So …

Things I Should Get Angry About

Jakub losing his job
William U
Anyone who's not allowed to sit on a bus
Women not getting the same rights as men
Children living in poverty around the world
only getting old egg sandwiches

Things It's Not OK to Get Angry About

Birthday parties (*that are actually quite good*)
Not spending INSECT day in front of the TV
(*because this INSECT day has actually been quite good*)
Polly (*who might actually be quite good*)
Being the Swedish Yule Goat (*which is actually quite a good part*)
Not getting sparkly flamingo pencils (*there's nothing actually quite good about this – I still really want one*)

That makes a lot of sense. So maybe I don't always need to stop being angry – maybe I need to use the right angry feelings in the right way.

And maybe I need to get more boxes.

174

CHaPTeR 26 ÷ 2

Today is the day of the Christmas Play and I am SUPER excited. Actually, the Swedish Yule Goat is quite a good part because I get to sing a solo, which makes me very excited and a bit nervous, so my tummy is full of those feelings and there isn't any room for angry bubbles too.

My dad has made me the BEST costume, so I look like a proper straw goat with my body sticking out of the top and my legs sticking out of the bottom. I look at

Freddie, whose mum put an old yellow pillowcase on his head to make him look like a deep-fried caterpillar from South Africa. I smile because I don't really know what to say about that.

You are only allowed two tickets to the play as there is only room in the hall for everyone to have two grown-ups in the audience. Dad let Granny have his ticket, but then Polly's mum Rita was really kind and gave him her extra one, so I'll have three adults at the play.

'That's not fair!' William U whined in class. 'I want three adults in the audience!'

'It's OK, William,' said William U's mum. 'I'm sure we can get an extra ticket, don't get upset ...'

'There are no more tickets,' said Ms Pitt-Bull firmly. 'How people choose to use their tickets is their business. Please make sure you are in the hall in your costumes promptly after lunchtime break.'

So that's where we are now – in the hall, waiting

for the play to start. Mr Spot, the school caretaker, has put up big curtains either side of the stage, so it looks like a proper theatre, and we're all peeking out to see if our grown-ups are there. I see Dad and Rita arrive together and he gives me a big wave – Rita must have given him a lift as well as a ticket, which is very nice of her. My granny is already sitting in her seat, but the space next to her is empty.

'I absolutely Pinky Promise I will be there,' Mum promised me this morning, linking our pinkies in the sacred vow. 'I have a big important meeting at lunch, but then I'll come straight to the play.'

'You Double Pinky Promise?' I said, holding out my other little finger.

'Double Pinky Promise,' Mum swore. A Pinky Promise is the most serious promise you can make. Sasha in Year 6's sister Megan told me that if you break a Pinky Promise, your nose will fall off and she's in Year 8 so it must be double true.

But the play starts in a few minutes and Mum still isn't here.

Our deputy head teacher, Ms De Promotion, comes to the front of the hall and the grown-ups go quiet. I look over at Granny. Still no Mum. Where is she?

'Welcome, everyone,' she says, 'to Year 5's wonderful Christmas Play! Miss Pelling sends her apologies that she cannot join us today – she's at an Executive Head Teacher Conference about the importance of good attendance.'

The adults all mumble. I think we might have another new head teacher soon.

'Year 5 have been working very hard to create this special occasion for you,' Ms De Promotion continues quickly, 'so let me hand straight over to the children to present … *The Star That Saved Christmas!*'

The parents clap and Mr Spot turns the lights

down and opens the curtains. Polly is standing in the centre of the stage and she's singing a song about how Christmas is in danger because of all the negative feelings in the world and she needs to raise everyone's Christmas spirits to save it. Polly sings it really well and she gets a big clap at the end. I join in too. A bit.

Now it's time to go through all the countries and everyone says their lines or sings a song. My Swedish Yule Goat part is quite near the end, so I look out into the audience again – my mum still isn't here. But she Pinky Promised, so she must be coming.

It's William U's turn and he's singing his Father Christmas song. William U doesn't sing well like Polly, but William U's mum thinks he does. I don't think the other parents are as excited as she is, even William U's dad who doesn't come to very many things and is doing something on his phone while

William U sings his song. If Ms Pitt-Bull catches him, she'll send him to The Cloud, or to Alcatraz, or whatever happens when parents break the rules at school.

William U is still singing his Father Christmas song, but he actually looks a bit sad that his dad isn't watching him. For once, I actually understand What Upset William. But he's not nearly as upset as William U's mum, who's doing that thing where she's still smiling, but she's also nudging William U's dad quite hard in the ribs too. But William U's dad is still doing the thing on his phone while William U sings.

William U finishes his song and looks at his dad, but his dad is still on his phone. So William U's mum takes the phone from William U's dad and makes him look at William U, which he does for nearly five whole seconds before he takes his phone back again. Everyone claps, but William U looks really upset and comes off the stage looking sad.

'Are you OK?' I ask him as he walks past.

'Of course I am – I got the best part, that's why my dad came,' William U snarls at me, wiping his nose with his red sleeve. His eyes look all pink and puffy. But I don't think it's an allergy this time.

'And at least my dad's here,' he says with a wobbly voice. 'Your mum can't even be bothered to turn up. So there!'

And with that he storms off. I look out at the parents again. He's right – there's still an empty seat next to my granny. And there isn't long – Vashti (*who brushed her hair specially, by the way*) is now singing about being a German pickle hidden in a Christmas tree and I'm next. Where is my mum?

'How are you feeling?' Maisie asks, coming and standing next to me in her tea towel. 'Are you worried?'

'No,' I say casually. 'My mum's going to be here.'

Maisie looks out to the audience and sees the empty chair.

'I meant about your song,' she says quietly.

'I knew that,' I say, even though I didn't.

Vashti finishes her song and Polly comes back on the stage. I start to feel my tummy bubbling. My mum promised she'd be here and she's not. Maybe she just needs a bit more time. That must be it! She just needs a bit more time …

I hear Polly say the line that means it's time for me to go onstage.

'And in Sweden, they celebrate Christmas with … the Swedish Yule Goat!'

That's when I'm supposed to walk on to the stage. But I need to give my mum a bit more time. So I don't go onstage. Polly looks confused.

'Oh, Swedish Yule Goat?' she cries out with a big smile. 'Where are you?'

I don't know what to say. This isn't in my lines.

 182

I don't do Stage Starz on Saturdays. Where would a goat be? What could a Swedish Yule Goat be doing that would make it late for Christmas? I need to think of something fast …

'Oh, Swedish Yule Goat!' Polly shouts again, sounding less happy this time. 'Where are you?'

I need inspiration. I look over at Freddie, who is crossing his legs – this is a very long time for him to be away from the boys' toilets. He must really …

A bell goes off. It's the one that always goes off at two o'clock for afternoon registration, but I also have an idea. I know what would be keeping the Swedish Yule Goat busy …

'OH, SWEDISH YULE GOAT?!' Polly screams, stamping her foot. 'WHERE ARE YOU?!'

'I'M HAVING A POO!' I shout back. That should give Mum a few more minutes. Certainly if the Swedish Yule Goat is anything like Freddie.

The adults start laughing. A lot.

'But ... but ... Swedish Yule Goat,' says Polly, looking at me as if she wants to make bad choices. 'You need to come out here and make all the people of Sweden feel the Christmas spirit!'

'I'll ... I'll ... I'll do it later,' I say, looking out into the audience, where there is still no sign of my mum.

The adults laugh again. Ms Pitt-Bull appears over the other side of the stage and gives me a Very Stern Look.

'But ... Swedish Yule Goat!' Polly shouts, looking very cross. 'We need to save Christmas! Now! Before home time!'

The adults are really laughing a lot now. (*Adults often laugh when things go wrong for children, by the way. But when they come out of the toilet and walk around for an hour with their skirt in their knickers, you're not allowed to find it funny at all. Just ask my mum about when we went to UniMingoes on Ice ...*)

'Swedish Yule Goat!' shouts Polly again. 'You need to come! Now!'

I look at Ms Pitt-Bull, who is giving me the Sternest Look Ever. It's no good. Mum or no Mum, I have to go out. I can feel the bubbly anger rising up in my tummy, even though the adults clap really hard as I come onstage. My dad gives me a massive wave and Granny gives me a big wink.

I start my song, but I can't stop the bubbles in my tummy. I look at the hall full of mums and dads and grannies and grandads and all the grown-ups who have come to support their special person and then I see the empty chair next to Granny. This isn't fair …

Oh no. Unfair. It's happening again.

I try to concentrate on my song and not the bubbles in my tummy. The music starts and it's time for me to sing, so I take a deep breath and try to remember all the words:

'I'm a goat, I'm made of straw,
And Christmas does excite me.
But please don't come to Gävle town
If you mean to ignite me.

You do not burn your Christmas tree
Or pumpkins on All Hallows.
I'm here to spread some Christmas cheer
And not to toast marshmallows.'

I finish the song and get a massive clap and cheer.
My dad stands up and punches the air (knocking
into William U's mum, by the way), and my granny
lets out a really formidable cheer, making the man
in front of her jump.

But I don't hear the clapping and the cheering. I
just see an empty chair.

Why isn't my mum here? Has she forgotten?

Like she forgot my sandwich? And my money for the wildlife park? And my playdate with Maisie? And …

The bubbles are so big now, I need them to go somewhere before they burst. I look at the big Christmas tree with our decorations on – it's starting to shake with all the balls filled with glitter and stars, but no one else can see it, as all the grown-ups who aren't my mum are facing me and I feel so angry that I think I might burst if I don't close my eyes and …

BOOOOOOOOOOM!

I hear a big gasp from the adults. That's it. Now everyone knows my secret. I'm in so much trouble.

I open my eyes and …

The room is filled with showers of glitter as the contents of all the baubles rain down on the audience, who ooh and ahh in delight. They clap and cheer some more. They think it was supposed

to happen and they are smiling.

But one person isn't smiling. My granny. She's looking at me very strangely indeed. I think I'm in trouble. But why would Granny be cross with me?

I run offstage and into the corridor. Maisie follows me and gives me a big hug.

'You were amazing!' she said. 'And no one cared about the exploding baubles, so it's all OK.'

'It's not OK!' I shout, angry tears coming down my face. 'My mum isn't here. I just wanted her to see me sing my song and she isn't even—'

'Your mum isn't he-re,' William U starts singing, 'your mum isn't he-re. Poor stupid Scarlett, her mum isn't he-re!'

I feel the bubbles rising up again.

'Scarlett, blow out your candles,' says Maisie, watching me get angrier.

'Are those for your fake cake?' William U says, 'because your mum can't be bothered to throw you

189

a real birthday party as well as not turn up for the Christmas Play …?'

I feel the bubbles about to explode. I close my eyes and …

'WILLIAM UNDERWOOD!' a stern voice shouts behind him.

William U freezes to the spot. I'm not sure he's ever been spoken to like that before. But even without looking around, he knows who it is.

'Yes, Ms Pitt-Bull?' he says, trying to sound all innocent.

'You need to apologise to Scarlett. Right now,' says Ms Pitt-Bull, her arms folded across her chest, which makes her look even crosser. Sasha from Year 6 says that once when Ms Pitt-Bull was parachuting from an aeroplane during the Wars of the Roses, she had to chop her own arm off and sew it back when it became stuck in her parachute. Those arms are tough.

'But I didn't do anything!' says William.

'I heard every last word,' says Ms Pitt-Bull. 'I wouldn't add lying to your list of bad choices.'

William U looks at me as if he hates me.

'Sorry, Scarlett,' he mumbles. He doesn't mean it.

'What you said was very, very unkind,' says Ms Pitt-Bull. 'In Rainbow Class we treat each other with respect.'

'What's going on?' says William U's mum, rushing up behind William and taking him in her arms. 'What's Upset William?'

'I'm afraid William has just made a very bad choice and was very unkind to Scarlett,' Ms Pitt-Bull explains.

'Oh, I'm sure there's a misunderstanding,' says William U's mum. 'My William's never unkind, are you, sweetie?'

'No,' says William, looking as if he's won. And

he probably has. His mum will help him to get away with it, like she always does ...

'Yes, he is,' says Ms Pitt-Bull simply. 'Just like all young people can be sometimes. And now he must face the consequences ...'

'Oh no,' says William U's mum, standing in front of William. 'William can't have consequences. He's ... allergic to them. He has ... Consequence Aversion Syndrome ...'

'I see,' says Ms Pitt-Bull, folding her arms again. 'I presume you have a letter from a qualified doctor confirming this diagnosis?'

'No,' whimpers William U's mum. 'But I read it on www.MyChildCentre.Universe. Twice.'

'Well, I'm afraid that is insufficient,' Ms Pitt-Bull declares. 'Let's finish the play. And then tomorrow, William, you will spend morning play on ... The Cloud!'

'NO!' cry William U and his mum together, as

if they've just been told that www.MyChildCentre. Universe has gone offline.

'Yes,' says Ms Pitt-Bull firmly. 'And I don't ever want to hear talk like that in my class again, William.'

'I ... I ... I'm going to talk to the governors about this!' William U's mum starts shrieking. 'This isn't right! I'm a teaching assistant in your class and—'

'Yes, I'm glad you brought that up,' says Ms Pitt-Bull, moving William U's mum away and talking to her quietly, but not so quietly that we can't hear. 'I've spoken to Miss Pelling and she agrees with me that this ... arrangement isn't working. From next term, you will be working with Ms Take in Reception Class instead.'

'No ... but ... I ...'

'You'll need to take it up with Miss Pelling. Although ... I believe she's at a conference on the Value of Spending Time With Your Staff next week,'

Ms Pitt-Bull says, coming back to Maisie and me. 'I suggest you return to the hall, William – it's nearly time for the finale.'

William U's mum stands frozen in the corridor as Ms Pitt-Bull takes Maisie and me back to the hall door.

'Now,' she says, looking at Maisie, 'you have been a very good friend, Maisie – and in Rainbow Class we look after each other. Have ten Positivity Points and return to the hall.'

Wow! Ten Positivity Points! That puts Maisie way top of the Positivity Chart. She'll be Star of the Week, so she gets Mr Nibbles this weekend. I'm really happy for her.

Kinda.

Maisie looks as if she wants to stay, but Ms Pitt-Bull has already held the door open and you don't want to argue with Ms Pitt-Bull. So Maisie looks at me and smiles as she goes back to the hall.

'Scarlett,' Ms Pitt-Bull says, turning her attention to me. 'You seem upset. Because your mother isn't here?'

It isn't really a question. But it is the right answer. I nod.

Ms Pitt-Bull looks at me.

'I understand,' she says. 'My mother worked when I was at school and she had to miss a lot of things. I often got very angry about it.'

I nod again, not sure if that's the right answer or if there even was a question.

'But the strange thing is,' she says, 'what I didn't understand until I became a mother was that it was just as hard for my mum. She never wanted to miss anything, but sometimes she had no choice. I'm sure your mum would much rather be here watching you than whatever she's doing today. And you still have two adults in the hall like all your friends. And they were incredibly proud of you.'

195

Wow! I can't believe it! I never thought about this before …

Ms Pitt-Bull has CHILDREN???!!! Sasha in Year 6 never said.

'I told you earlier in the term that your mother had written to me about your temper,' Ms Pitt-Bull carries on. 'So I've been watching you very closely and …'

Oh no. She's figured it out. She knows that it's me who is making things explode. I'm going to spend the rest of my life on The Cloud …

'I've been very impressed with how you've been trying to handle your anger. Well done, Scarlett.'

'What?' I say before I can stop it. 'I mean, pardon?'

Ms Pitt-Bull smiles. ACTUALLY smiles. It's weird. But kinda nice.

'I said I'm impressed,' she says. 'Changing ourselves is something everyone Finds a Challenge.

And you're working very hard to do that. It's very impressive and I think you should be rewarded. Now about Mr Nibbles …'

Oh wow! She's going to let me have Mr Nibbles this weekend! But that would mean taking him from Maisie and I don't want to do that. Not really. Not totally. Not much …

'As you know, someone needs to care for Mr Nibbles every weekend,' says Ms Pitt-Bull. 'But

someone also needs to care for him over the Christmas holidays. For two weeks. Do you think … you might be able to do that?'

I feel my heart start to puke a bit in my chest. Two whole weeks with Mr Nibbles! **TWO WHOLE WEEKS WITH MR NIBBLES!!!**

'YES!' I shout, even though I don't mean to. 'I mean – I've got a whole area ready for him with a bed and an obstacle course and a book and …'

'Excellent,' says Ms Pitt-Bull, opening the hall door a crack and smiling. 'Well, then that's settled. Keep up the good work, Scarlett. You're doing very well. Now go back to the stage so you don't miss the big finale. I think someone is very keen to see you …'

She opens the door and points to the back of the hall. There's my mum all hot and sweaty and with her hair like a bird sat in it. She made it! I go out onstage and we sing our finale and all the parents clap. My mum is smiling, but it's a sad smile. I think she's sad she missed my song.

But then Ms Pitt-Bull comes onstage, brings me to the front and starts the music for my Swedish Yule Goat song again. Everyone cheers and my mum smiles a proper big smile.

So I get to sing it again and this time I'm happy because my mum is there and everyone claps along and when I finish, everyone gives me a massive cheer, but I think my mum is probably cheering the loudest out of everyone and I give her a big smile so she knows I'm not cross with her and as she sits in the empty seats where William U's mum and dad were I think she's happy crying a bit. This is the BEST.

I might not have got the main part in the play, but now I feel like a star.

The Star That Saved Mr Nibbles for Christmas.

CHAPTER 10 + 4

One of the good things about when parents make a mistake is that they work **REALLY SUPER** hard to make it up to you. Mum felt so bad about being so late for the play (*it turned out that her meeting ran really late, then the car broke down AGAIN, by the way, so it really wasn't her fault at all – and after I've had all my treats, I'll make sure I tell her that*), she said I was allowed sweeties **AND** screen time again, so Granny could give me the big bag of sweets that she'd brought just in case, then we all sat down with Jakub and watched the performance of the play that the school had filmed on the Big Telly with popcorn **AND** a takeaway pizza, so Mum got to see it all anyway.

The adults said that while everyone was very good and had worked really hard, I was especially good, and they all agreed so that's fair like a vote and they must be right.

As an extra special treat, Granny got to read me my story and put me to bed, so we read my favourite book called *The Girl Who Lost Her Sparkle*, which Mum always says is too long, but Granny read the **WHOLE** book.

Now it's nearly time for sleep, but instead of turning the light off, Granny goes to my bedroom door and closes it gently, staying on the inside.

'Scarlett,' she says, 'I want to talk to you about what happened today.'

'It's OK,' I say, trying not to yawn. Popcorn and pizza are really tiring. 'I understand that Mum has to Make Ends Meet and that the silly man in the garage who didn't fix the car properly is a total—'

'Not that,' says Granny, sitting on the edge of

201

the bed. 'The other thing.'

'What other thing?' I ask her because I don't
know what she's talking about, probably because
she was born in the 1940s and she is talking in
olden days talk.

She looks at me.

'The … exploding thing,' she says quietly. 'I
know that was you.'

Oh no!

How does she know? Will she tell Mum? Will she tell the newspapers? Will she send me to a lab for scientists to give me injections? Will she take her sweets away …?

'It's all right,' she says. 'I understand. Your secret is safe with me.'

Phew. But how does she …?

'But how do you know?' I ask her, as it makes more sense to ask her than ask the question inside my head because I know my head doesn't have the answer in it.

She holds my hand and leans forward.

'Because it used to happen to me,' she whispers. 'My **BIG FEELINGS** made strange things happen too.'

I'm very glad my tummy is full of pizza and popcorn and sweets because otherwise I think I'd puke in surprise.

'What?' I ask to be sure I haven't misunderstood

and 'made strange things happen' didn't mean something different in the 1940s, like 'that isn't cricket', 'jolly hockey sticks' and 'text' did.

'My **BIG FEELINGS** used to make strange things happen,' she repeats. 'So when I was angry, I made things explode. Just like you did today.'

'Wow,' I said, sitting up. 'Well … how did you stop it? I'm so worried about the wedding and spoiling Aunty Rosa and Aunty Amara's day and that I won't get to go to Super Mega Awesome Sicky Fun World and—'

Granny raises a hand. That meant 'be quiet' in the 1940s.

'I grew up in very different times to these,' she says.

'I know,' I say. 'You only had one phone in the whole world and you had to go to a special shop if you wanted to rent a movie, which was really hard because they hadn't invented televisions yet.'

'Sort of,' Granny smiles. 'Let's come back to that another time. But when I was young, I grew up in a family where people weren't allowed to have **BIG FEELINGS**. Especially if you were a little girl.'

I can feel my tummy bubbling. It might be because it's totally unfair when girls are expected to behave differently to boys. Or it might be because of the fifth slice of Pepperoni Delight I ate.

'So I was told never to express my feelings,' says Granny. 'I was told to push them down and never let them out. But that's just silly. You can't stop feeling something. Any more than you can stop the sun from shining, or the sea from flowing. Or ...'

'... slime from coming out of a party bag,' I say to help her.

'Quite,' Granny agrees. 'So what I found was that the more I tried to keep my feelings in, the more they tried to come out another way. I made all kinds of things explode – my brother's model aeroplane collection, my grandmother's sherry trifle … and it took a long time to forget one unfortunate incident with our outside toilet …'

A little giggle comes out. Granny exploded poo too. That makes me feel better.

'So how did you stop it?' I ask her.

'As I grew older and I found my own voice, I started to make choices that made me less angry,' Granny continues. 'My parents wanted me to get married when I was eighteen, but I secretly went and sat the exams to go to university – and I passed them. There I discovered new ways to express myself – and once I learned to communicate my feelings, there were far fewer explosions. Although it doesn't always work. You just ask that man in the post office when he barged in front of me last week. He picked a bad day to buy a new pillow …'

I giggle again. Granny is so cool. For an old person who thinks a text is something in a book.

'There are lots of ways of dealing with anger,' Granny says. 'But the most important thing is to tell someone about it. You'll find you feel a lot better for it. Why don't you start with me?'

And so I tell her about all the things that have made me angry lately … Mum cancelling my party, forgetting the stuff for my school trip, not organising Maisie's playdate …

'I just feel as if Mum is too busy for me,' I say. 'I understand that she has to Make Ends Meet because Jakub can't find his job, but that's not my fault. And things keep going wrong for me because of it.'

'I see,' says Granny, nodding wisely. 'You need to talk to your mum about this. She'd be very sad to know you feel this way.'

'Well, that's why I can't tell her!' I say. 'She's so stressedy and worriedy and upsety all the time, if I tell her this, it will make it worse. She might start cooking.'

Granny takes my hand again.

'You're right,' she says. 'Your mum is under a lot of pressure at the moment and all those things are important. But believe me. None of them are as important as you. You have to talk to her. She always has time for you.'

I look at Granny as if I'm not sure. This needs some more thought.

'While you're thinking about it, I've brought someone who might help,' she says, pulling something out of her bag. It's an old teddy bear. I can tell it's old because it actually looks like a bear, not a unicorn or a llama or the things teddy bears usually look like. It's very old. But I like it.

'This is Barney,' she says, giving him to me. He's very soft and I give him a big cuddle. 'I used to talk to him when I was upset. He's an excellent listener.'

'He's a stuffed bear,' I point out.

'That's probably why,' says Granny. 'I thought

perhaps you might like to talk to him too?'

I look at Barney. Now I'm ten, I'm really far too grown up for teddies. But if it would make Granny happy, I'll keep him. He can keep the other twenty-four teddies in my bed company.

'Now,' says Granny, giving me a kiss on my head. 'It's time for you to go to sleep.'

'OK,' I say, my head full of very busy thoughts.

Granny pauses.

'But before you do,' she whispers, with a naughty smile, climbing on to the bed next to me, 'do you want to hear about the time I exploded your great-grandmother's lumpy gravy all over everyone at our Christmas dinner …?'

ChAPTER 30÷2

Today is the day of Aunty Rosa and Aunty Amara's wedding and I'm excited, nervous, scared, happy, worried and a bit pukey all at the same time. I've had my hair done all pretty and Mum says I might even be allowed to wear a tiny bit of lip gloss as it's a SUPER SPECIAL DAY. But what I'm not allowed to do is put my dress on until five minutes before the wedding because Mum says that I'll get it dirty and she's probably totally right.

We're in my aunties' Big Posh House where they are getting married and everyone is running around doing wedding stuff. The cooking people are just bringing in the massive wedding cake – well, really it's **FOUR** cakes all on top of each other and each one's a different flavour. Aunty Rosa let me choose, so I chose white chocolate, milk chocolate, dark chocolate and vanilla in case anyone doesn't like chocolate (*although that's the smallest cake, by the way, because it's not chocolate*).

But the wedding cake makes me very worried. What if William U winds me up? What if I lose my temper? What if I explode cake all over the wedding? What if …?

I think back to my conversation with Granny. I need to talk to someone, but everyone is super busy with the wedding. But I did bring Barney with me, just in case someone much younger than me who isn't too old for teddies wants him. I sit him down on the table in front of me.

'So, Barney,' I tell him. I feel a bit silly talking to a bear, but Mum says that talking to Jakub is sometimes like talking to a brick wall, so it can't be any sillier than that. 'I'm a bit worried about this wedding. I want Aunty Rosa and Aunty Amara to have the bestest day ever, ever, but I don't want to spoil it with my temper. You see, there's quite a lot I'm angry about. I'm angry that Jakub lost his job – not with Jakub because it's not his fault he got the wrong sort of sack and I love him lots like jelly tots, and he didn't really lose his job, someone took it away from him, which is like when Callum who left to live in Canada took my pencil sharpener in Year 2 and everyone said I'd lost it, but he had it in his pencil case and he was stupid. I got a new pencil sharpener, but I'm worried Jakub won't get a new job and then we won't be able to have good stuff like Pizza Fridays and Mum will have to work all the time to Make Ends Meet and she'll keep on forgetting Important Things like cheese sandwiches and sparkly flamingo pencils and then maybe she and Jakub will get an angry divorce like Kevin's mum and dad did and she'll be really sad and even though I'll get two trampolines, I won't live with Jakub any more and then—'

'Oh, Scarlett!'

Wow. Barney's lips didn't even move. And he sounds exactly like my mum. That's weird …

I feel a warm pair of arms around me and the smell of Special Perfume for Big Days and it's my mum and she's giving me the biggest hug ever. She sits down at the table.

'Baby girl ... why didn't you tell me any of this?' she says, holding my face.

I look at Barney. Granny was right. He's good.

'Because ... you're always busy and stressedy and grumpy and I don't want to make you grumpier and stressedier,' I say honestly.

'Oh, my love,' she says, bringing me into a big hug. 'I've always got time for you. No matter how grumpy and ... stressedy I am ... I know it's been a tricky few months, but it's all going to be fine. We've got each other and we've got our friends and ... well, I felt so bad when Ms Pitt-Bull told me I'd forgotten your money for the wildlife park, I went and got this ...'

She pulls something out of her Handbag for Posh. I gasp.

'A sparkly flamingo pencil!' I shriek, giving her a big hug. My mum is the actual **BEST**.

Now she just needs to get me the candy cane and

 214

the monkey rubber.

'I love you, Scarlett Fife,' says Mum. 'It's all going to be OK, I promise …'

'**WE'VE WON!!!**' comes a huge shout from the other side of the room. '**WE'VE WOOOOOOOONNNNNNN!!!!**'

Aunty Rosa comes running over with a phone in one hand and a super happy Jakub in the other.

'What?' says Mum, her eyes getting a bit soggy.

'Pardon,' I correct her.

'**WE'VE WON!**' says Jakub, picking Mum up and spinning her around and she doesn't even tell him he's an eejit or a wally and they hug and then they pick me up and spin me around and they hug Aunty Rosa, even though she's only in a dressing gown and then Aunty Amara comes running in and she's in a dressing gown too and Granny comes in and shouts because the brides aren't supposed to see each other, but they don't care and everyone just

dances around and I think it's a good time to ask a
question.

'What have we won?' I ask, hoping it's the school
Christmas raffle and I got the massive stuffed rabbit

that everyone wants.

'The court case!' says Jakub, kneeling down and hugging me. 'We won my court case!'

Oh. Right. That's good too.

'The judge agreed with us – Gary is going to have to pay you all the money he owes you, plus some more to say sorry,' says Aunty Rosa, as Aunty Amara picks me up and gives me a massive kiss. 'It turns out that lots of other people have complained too, so he's in loads of trouble. But we won!'

Mum gives Aunty Rosa a huge hug and they cry a bit and it's nice to see them being friends for a change.

Mum holds me and kisses my pretty hair.

'You see – it's all going to be OK,' she says. 'And do you know what the best thing is?'

'The massive stuffed rabbit?' I ask hopefully.

'Er … no,' she says, looking a bit confused. 'Tomorrow we get to go … TO SUPER MEGA

217

AWESOME SICKY FUN WORLD!!! LAST ONE ON THE GUTS-A-CHURNO COASTER IS A ROTTEN EGG SANDWICH!!'

Everyone laughs and dances around and they are super happy, even when Aunty Amara realises she's left her curling irons on and she and Jakub run upstairs with a fire extinguisher before she sets the house on fire like the dinner ladies did with the fish fingers.

Aunty Rosa walks past a table and takes William U's and his mum's and dad's name places off the table.

'Why are you doing that?' I ask her.

'Oh, they called this morning, they can't make it,' she says. 'Apparently William has come out in an allergic reaction to something.'

'Discipline?' says my mum not very quietly. It must be a vegetable. Sounds worse than broccoli.

Everyone goes back to hugging and kissing and

218

dancing around. It's great to see my family so super happy and excited. Today's going to be a brilliant day where we celebrate love and family and happiness.

The giant stuffed rabbit would have been nice, though.

Weddings are **SUPER** awesome. Aunty Rosa and Aunty Amara stood in front of all their family and friends – apart from William U and his parents – and promised to love each other for always and everyone cried even though they were happy and then we all ate loads of nice food and danced to a real band with trumpets. Maisie was allowed to come as my special friend for the evening and everyone gave us the little bags of sweets on all the tables and now we're eating them until we're nearly sick.

'So do you think you're going to be OK now?' says Maisie as we sit under a table and share our sweeties.

'Most of the time,' I say. 'I think it's OK to be angry sometimes. And sometimes it isn't. And sometimes you can't help it. And sometimes you can control it. And sometimes you can't. But you should talk about it. And things like bears and hamsters help.'

'*Case a raspberry, case a raspberry,*' Maisie says. 'That's French for "stuff happens" … Oh, I meant to tell you, your dad's looking for you – he just arrived when I was getting these from your Great-Aunty Pat.'

'Cool,' I say, climbing out from under the table to go and find him. I want him to see my beautiful dress, even though it's not quite as beautiful as it was this morning as I spilt a bit of blackcurrant juice down it. And a jam sandwich. And a lollipop. And some fire from a candle (*but the blackcurrant juice put it out, by the way*).

I look around at all the adults dancing on the dance floor – it's so sweet watching grown-ups dance, they try so hard. I expect Dad to be there Finding Dancing a Challenge, biting his bottom lip and shaking his bum a lot, but he's not. But I do recognise someone on the opposite side of the dance floor.

It's Polly. What is she doing at my aunties' wedding? We haven't really become friends yet, so I'm not sure if I'm very happy about this. But looking at her grumpy face, neither is she ...

'Hey, sprout!' says Dad, dancing up behind me. 'Wow! You look amazing! Love the blackcurrant!'

He picks me up and gives me a big tickly kiss, making me giggle.

'So ...' he says, looking all shiny and excited. I haven't seen him like this for ages. It's nice. He must be happy about Jakub's court case too. 'There's someone I want to introduce you to ... my new girlfriend!'

'Wow!' I say, super pleased that he's found someone. I just hope she likes his carpet. 'Where is she?'

At that moment, Polly's mum Rita steps up,

which is a bit annoying as she's right in the way of me seeing Dad's new girlfriend. I try to look around her, but Dad pulls me back.

'Er … squidge,' he says. 'She's right here. I know you already know her, but, Scarlett … please let me formally introduce my new girlfriend … Rita!'

Rita holds out her hand with a big smile.

'It's wonderful to meet you properly, Scarlett,' she says. 'I can't wait to get to know you better.'

I look at Dad. He's joking, right?

But as Polly comes up behind them, I can see this is no joke. I feel the bubbles rising in my stomach, just as the cake is brought out for my aunties to cut. I look at it, trying not to think about my dad making Polly's mum his girlfriend.

'Scarlett?' says Dad, as I shut my eyes to try to keep the bubbles down. 'Scarlett? Scarlett …?'

KERRRRRRSPLLLAAAAT!

I don't need to open my eyes this time.

I just really hope everyone likes chocolate cake …

Acknowledgements

I have had the BEST fun writing this book and I'm so grateful to everyone at Hachette for letting me come and play in their sandpit. Special thanks go to my editor Rachel Wade for asking me in for a coffee and sending me home with a book deal – beats a stale custard cream any day.

I am indebted to Dominique Valente, author of the fantastic *Starfell* series, for her time and stellar feedback. Thanks so much, Dominique – sorry to have distracted you, please get back to writing more brilliant books.

This book is dedicated to Veronique Baxter, who has been my constant friend, advisor and counsellor for the past five years – and has somehow managed to find time to be my agent too. You are a bright star by which to navigate this voyage, V – I am so, so blessed to have you.

In this, as in all things, I must thank my beautiful patchwork family for their boundless love and support, even when I explode. Johnny, Ian, Zach, Lili and Dilly, I love you with all that I am – and I'll try much harder not to burn the Blackeroni Cheese.

Finally, my enormous thanks to you, my brilliant readers – I am nothing without you. Well, that's not entirely true – without you, I'd be a strange old lady writing words by herself in a slightly smelly room. So I'd rather keep you, if that's OK? I hope you enjoy these new adventures with Scarlett Fife – I'd love to see you next time.

Much love – stay groovy,
Maz
xxx